# THE LAKE MURRAY MURDERS

## STEVEN JACOBS

# OTHER WORKS BY THE AUTHOR

# OTHER WORKS

# THE LAKE MURRAY MURDERS

Work of Fiction
By: Steven Jacobs

# DEDICATIONS

A big THANK YOU to two coworkers, G.B. and E.J., for your help.

*"I'm not working on The Great American Novel. All I'm doing, I hope, is entertaining readers."*
*Clive Cussler*

# PROLOGUE

Atlanta, Georgia, 1960

Using fraudulent documents, the ringleader of a three-man group procured a room at a low-end motel two weeks before. He had picked this particular motel for a specific reason. It was off the beaten path and the kind of place where people kept to themselves.

The group stayed in the room as much as possible to avoid being spotted, and when they went out, it was only for food or supplies, and then it was right back to the motel room. Finally, though, their stay at the seedy motel was coming to an end.

The three men spent the better part of their last afternoon in the motel wiping down the room and getting rid of any papers that could be linked back to them. While the ringleader went through the room with a proverbial fine-tooth comb, the other two men loaded a van procured by the ringleader using the same fraudulent documents used to rent the room. This meticulous detail kept the ringleader from getting caught for years and landed him on the top of the FBI's most wanted list for an art thief. He was a thorn in the side of the art community. Tonight's score, however, would be his final and biggest score yet. Tonight, he would be going out with a bang.

After the two men finished loading the van, the ringleader checked out of the motel in the dead of night without incident, then walked out to the van and hopped into the driver's seat.

The ringleader, known only to the other two men as Mr. Washington, asked, "Are you ready, boys?"

"Sure, we're ready," one of the men said.

"Yeah. Ready to start spending all that money!" The other man said.

"Don't spend it yet. We still have a long way to go," Mr. Washington replied flatly. As he cranked up the van and pulled out of the parking lot, Mr. Washington said, "Let's go over it again while you two put your overalls on."

While the two men got suited up, they went over the plan they had come up with on the half-hour drive into the city. "We'll drive into town, where we will park in the alley on the other side of the building beside the museum," the man named Mr. Adams replied.

Immediately, the other man, named Mr. Jefferson, picked up where Adams left off, saying, "Using the fire escape, we will make our way up to the roof, where we will cross over to the museum roof using the rope system."

"Exactly," Mr. Washington replied, "Once we're on the roof of the museum, I will gain access through the skylight that's under repair and unguarded. Then I'll rope down and take the guards out. After that, it's easy pickings from there, but we'll have to work quickly to get as many pieces out in the time frame as we can."

"We understand our parts, and it should go off smoothly as long as you can take care of the two guards," Mr. Jefferson said smugly.

"I'll take care of my part. You two just be ready when I give that rope a first tug," Mr. Washington replied.

Twenty minutes later, Mr. Washington slowly circled the eerily vacant block where the museum was located and entered a narrow alley one building over from the museum. After sitting for a moment, Mr. Washington got out and walked to the end of the alleyway to look around. Glancing at his watch, it read 02:30. Once he was sure the roads were empty, Mr. Washington returned to the van, where the three men sprang into action, saying, "All right, let's move. We have ninety minutes!"

With ropes, tools, and specially made loot bags, all three men climbed quietly and efficiently onto the fire escape from the van and made their way to the roof of the vacant property.

Once they gained access to the roof, all three men crossed over to the opposite side of the building to the alleyway separating the building they were on from the museum. Working with the speed of a NASCAR pit crew, the three men threw a rope over using the tried-and-true grappling hook method.

Once the rope was secure, Mr. Washington pulled himself across the rope to the museum's rooftop using a pulley attached to his harness. Moments later, he was standing on the museum's rooftop and uncoupling from the rope he used to cross over from the adjacent building. After uncoupling, he flashed a dim light across the alley to the other two accomplices. Then, he watched as Mr. Adams got on the rope and crossed over to the museum's rooftop.

Working quickly, Mr. Washington and Mr. Adams quietly moved to the unprotected skylight under repairs and, using a series of suction cups and a glass cutter, removed a section of glass, giving Mr. Washington access to the museum's interior.

Moments later, Mr. Washington started to repel down into the museum from the skylight. Without making a sound, he stopped repelling when he was still ten feet off the ground to ensure the coast was clear. While momentarily stopped, he glanced at his watch to ensure they were on schedule, which they were.

With his feet firmly on the ground inside the locked museum, Mr. Washington looked at his watch, now read 02:55. He had precisely five minutes before one of the guards made their last rounds and one hour until the next set of fresh guards came on duty.

Mr. Washington picked this precise time because he knew the two guards would be nearing the end of their shift, and by this time, they would be tired and sleepy. Mr. Washington silently pulled the lead-filled sap from his backpack, melted into the shadows, and waited for the guard to make his rounds.

The museum was as quiet as a tomb while he waited in the shadow by the door for the guard to enter. At this point, even the slightest noise could give him away. Suddenly, Mr. Washington heard footsteps.

Mr. Washington held his breath as the guard unlocked the door to the locked wing and walked in. Dressed entirely in black with blackout makeup on his face, the guard walked past Mr. Washington without seeing him. When the guard stepped into the room and was out of sight of the main guard post, the ringleader struck, knocking the guard out with a single blow to the back of the head.

Acting quickly, Mr. Washington wrapped his arms around the guard to ease him to the ground so the noise didn't arouse the second guard's suspicion until the first guard was tied up. After taking a moment to tie up the guard, the blacked-out figure took the radio off the guard's side and keyed the transmit button, saying just two words, "Come here," hoping the second guard wouldn't notice his voice was different than the other guards with just two words.

The ruse worked, and the second guard entered the wing moments later. Like the first guard, the second guard never stood a chance, and in moments, he was laid out beside his comrade, knocked out cold, tied up, and gagged.

Now free and clear of guards, Mr. Washington ran back to the skylight and flashed the small flashlight straight up at his accomplice on the roof, who had already begun lowering specially made loot bags that fit into the hole left by the glass they had just cut out of the skylight. Working feverishly, Mr. Washington removed piece after piece of artwork off the mountings of the museum, knowing the woefully inadequate alarm system was only on the doors and windows and there were no pressure switches on the artwork themselves.

Working as quickly as possible, Mr. Washington would pull the pieces off the wall and fill the basket as rapidly as possible. Mr. Adams then pulled the basket up, moved the pieces to the rope across the alley, and fed the pieces over to the adjacent building. From there, Mr. Jefferson took the pieces off the rope and returned the basket to

Mr. Adams. While Mr. Adams was retrieving the basket and returning it to the skylight, Mr. Jefferson moved the pieces across the adjacent building on the roof nearest the getaway van.

In this way, the three men formed an ad hoc bucket brigade, steadily moving pieces out of the museum for the next forty minutes. Finally, with twenty minutes to the guard change, Mr. Adams pulled Mr. Washington back up the rope, but not before Mr. Washington left a business card with one word on it ... Erebus.

With all three men safely off the museum property, they quickly lowered their haul to the awaiting van. As they lowered the last basket to the ground, Mr. Adams saw the relief guards showing up for work. Mr. Washington said, "We gotta move! It won't take those guards long to figure out something's wrong when their buddies don't show up to let them inside!"

Loading the last pieces frantically, all three men piled into the van and slowly pulled out of the alleyway as they heard an alarm blaring nearby.

Later that day, a local fire department got reports of a van on fire along a back country road outside of Atlanta. After the fire was extinguished, the bodies of two individuals were found in the back. Police and FBI responded, hoping this van had something to do with the museum break-in the night before. The FBI went over the area with a proverbial fine-toothed comb. Still, no trace of the perpetrator was ever discovered other than the Erebus calling card left in the museum. To make matters worse, the stolen artwork, including a Cézanne, a Renoir, and a van Gogh, among other valuable pieces, were never recovered.

This would be the fourteenth and last calling card found by various authorities over the years. As quickly as he descended on the art theft scene, Erebus disappeared. Not only was he never apprehended, but nobody really knew his nationality or even if he was a male or female, for that matter. Erebus was a total ghost.

～

LAKE MURRAY, South Carolina, 1990

Sam eased out of bed before the sun appeared early one Saturday morning, being ever so mindful not to wake his wife of twenty years. He picked up the clothes he had laid out the previous night and walked into the bathroom to change.

After changing and brushing his teeth, Sam walked out of the bathroom and went into the kitchen to make a pot of fresh coffee. While waiting for the coffee to finish brewing, he grabbed a snack and fixed himself a few sandwiches for the fishing trip.

As quietly as possible, Sam eased out of the house and hopped into his truck, which already had his boat hooked up to it and ready to go, hoping for a nice quiet day of fishing with his best friend Henry, whom he was meeting for breakfast at their usual Waffle House.

After meeting his friend of many years and having a quiet breakfast, the two headed for Lake Murray to start their relaxing day on the lake fishing. The pair had been fishing in the shallower waters off Pine Island to no avail just after the sun came up when the duo decided to move into deeper waters closer to the dam.

Since there was still quite a bit of fog hanging about the area, they motored slowly toward the well-known intake towers that rose out of the water near the earthen dam. Before Sam cut his engine, he and Henry could make out another boat's silhouette in the distant fog.

"Looks like someone beat us out here already," Sam said as they slowly motored into a position near one of the towers.

"Seems like it," Henry replied, eying the other boat warily.

"Do you see something?" Sam asked, noticing that Henry hadn't yet taken his eyes off the boat since it came into view.

"Something's not right," Henry replied, not taking his eyes off the boat.

"What are you talking about?" Sam asked.

"There's nobody aboard that boat," Henry said, "and it's not tied off or anything. It looks like it's drifting."

"I think you need another cup of coffee," Sam said with a chuckle.

"No, I'm serious. I can't see anybody aboard," Henry shot back from the boat's bow.

"Okay, fine. Let's ease our way on over and have a look. If that's the case and nobody is aboard, maybe it broke free from a dock overnight and somehow ended up here. I'm going to cut the motor back here. Fire up the trolling motor, and let's ease over to her."

Henry steered the trolling motor towards the boat, and as the pair got closer, the details of the boat emerged through the thinning fog. Henry could tell it was a smaller fiberglass boat with perhaps a ten-horsepower outboard motor on the back but not much else.

This boat reminded Henry of the small dingy boats usually pulled behind a sailboat used for motoring back and forth to shore. However, something was different about this boat.

As Henry motored closer and closer to the boat, he began to see streaks of red along the edge and running down the outside hull of the boat. "Whadda ya see?" Sam asked from the back.

As Henry eased their boat up to the seemingly unoccupied and adrift boat, he suddenly drew back and shouted, "HOLY MOTHER OF GOD! There's a body in here!"

"What are you talking about?" Sam asked, suspecting Henry of trying to pull a fast one on him. Sam grabbed a flashlight from the back of his boat and went to where Henry was in the bow. Standing beside Henry, Sam flicked his flashlight on and peered into the boat.

As soon as the flashlight's beam landed on the interior of the mystery boat, both men gasped at the ghastly sight before them. Lying at the bottom of the boat near the stern was the crumpled figure of a man's body. Judging by the amount of bloody handprints, blood smears, and the pool of blood near the body and the body's ashen color, there could be no doubt he was dead.

"DON'T TOUCH ANYTHING!" Sam shouted.

"Do you think I'm stupid or something?" Henry snapped back as he frantically reversed the trolling motor and got some distance between the two boats. "What are we going to do?"

Sam asked, "Do you have one of those newer phones that can fit in your pocket?"

Henry replied smartly, "Hell no! I'm sixty-eight and retired. What in the hell do I need a phone for?"

"Neither do I! Well, crank up the motor, then we gotta go back to call the police!" Sam shot back.

"I'm way ahead of ya," Henry said as he started back toward the console of his boat. Moments later, Henry shouted, "Better hang on!" Not long after that, the boat carrying Henry and Sam rocketed across the lake back to the boat landing so they could call for help.

Over the next several hours, Henry and Sam learned the man's name was Jonathon Blackwood. He was a man from a well-off local family in Irmo. Both men followed the case on the news and in the local newspaper; however, after quite some time, the case grew cold.

Police eventually linked Jonathon Blackwood to another person named Peter Harrington, Jonathon's longtime friend who had died a short time before under mysterious circumstances. Still, nothing ever came from it, and nobody was ever arrested in Jonathon Blackwood's murder.

# 1

**T**he Present

Detective Drew Clayton from the Lexington County Sheriff's Department parked in the parking lot of the now roped-off boat dock. Thankfully, it was early morning, and only a few trucks with empty trailers were in the lot.

Yawning and taking a sip of his steaming hot coffee before he got out, Clayton said, "I'm not going to miss these early morning calls after I retire."

Clayton hopped out and stretched out his back before reaching back into the car and retrieving two coffee cups, one for him and the other for his partner, Detective Amy Stone, who had arrived on the scene before he did.

As Clayton walked through the parking lot toward the boat dock, he could tell this would not be an ordinary case. The closer he got to the boat landing, he could see a South Carolina Department of Natural Resources boat offshore, keeping nosy boaters away from the landing and the nearby dock. As he walked along the small footpath past the boat landing and towards a small dock, he could see a boat tied up to the floating dock, and several crime scene technicians were taking photos and fingerprints of the boat.

Clayton's partner, Detective Amy Stone, was the polar opposite of him. Young, attractive, and energetic, she had gotten her detective shield the previous year and was looking forward to moving into the next phase of her career.

On the other hand, Clayton was old enough to be her father, if not her grandfather. He had started out as a beat cop twenty years before Stone was born and worked his way through the ranks. This was to be Clayton's last year before retiring, and earlier in the year, the higher-ups had stuck him with a rookie detective.

At first, Clayton didn't like her, not one bit, but after working on several smaller cases, Clayton saw that Stone had a unique way of looking at things and, due to the generational gap, had proven herself very useful in the art of information gathering via, Facebook, Instagram, and other social media platforms.

Stone saw Clayton coming and met him halfway down the dock, where he handed her a cup of steaming coffee and asked, "What do we have?"

Stone thanked Clayton for the coffee and took a sip before answering, "One victim with an apparent gunshot wound to the chest. Photographs, measurements, and sketches have already been done, and the crime scene guys say there's no wallet or ID with the body. There is, however, blood all over the boat. The coroner said the victim died sometime in the overnight hours. The examiner is standing by to remove the body, but I wanted you to see the victim first."

Stone took another sip of her coffee and said, "Fisherman found the boat adrift out in the lake right before the sun came up and called 911. It took some time, but a sheriff's boat arrived and got the ball rolling."

"Well, let's have a look. Shall we?" Clayton said as they walked the rest of the way down the dock to the tied-up boat.

As he walked up, Clayton could see blood smears and bloody handprints all around the boat, but mainly around the back of the boat and on the outboard boat motor throttle handle.

The young woman's body was lying face up in the bottom of the boat in a pool of her own blood. One of the first things Clayton saw was the cross tattoo on her inside wrist. They could also see a bloody rag had been stuffed under her long-sleeve shirt near the wound in an apparent attempt to staunch the bleeding to no avail. Clayton also noted that the young woman's shirt and pants were torn in several places, indicating she was frantic to get away and possibly ran through some woods at one point.

Clayton stood momentarily staring at the boat, then said, "Somebody must have been chasing her."

"How can you tell?" Stone asked.

Without answering the question directly, Clayton asked, "Do you know anything about boats?"

"No. Why?"

"Luckily for you, I lived near the coast as a kid and went fishing in the intercoastal waterway all the time in boats like this one. Look at where the majority of the blood smears are. What do you see?"

Stone looked the boat over and replied, "There are blood splotches near the front of the boat, then drops of blood and more smears across the bench seat, trailing back to the back of the boat, where ..."

"Exactly," Clayton said as he finished her sentence, "she had to untie the boat and crank the engine."

Stone watched Clayton closely examine the boat's stern, then said, "Ya see that red tank in the back by the motor? That's the fuel tank. What ya wanna bet it's empty?"

"No bet," Stone said as she watched Clayton intently.

Clayton asked the crime scene photographer if he had a picture of the boat's oar, which he had, so Clayton donned a pair of gloves and, being ever so careful not to disturb any of the blood evidence, gingerly picked up the oar and gave the fuel tank a little tap and a nudge.

"Sounds empty, and I'm pretty sure it shouldn't move that easy," Stone said.

"Exactly," Clayton replied. "Apparently, somebody chased her out onto a dock and either shot her on the dock or after she had already gotten in the boat trying to get away. From the looks of her clothes, she ran through the woods also."

"Either way, she was hit and managed to get out into the lake, where she ran out of fuel and then slowly bled out," Stone replied sadly.

Clayton said, "Now the real questions begin."

"Exactly. Who was she? Where and why was she killed?" Stone asked aloud to nobody in particular.

Detective Clayton said sadly, "Ok, release the body to the coroner, and let's figure out who this girl is."

"And just how are we going to do that?" Stone asked as she watched Clayton squat down at the boat's bow and take a picture of the boat's required registration number.

"Well, the first thing we're going to do while we're waiting for the coroner's report is we are going to check with the Department of Natural Resources to see who this boat is registered to. That will hopefully give us a good starting point. After that, we'll check in with the coroner later to see if they have anything for us."

The pair stayed at the boat dock for another hour before the two wrapped up at the crime scene. Stone's stomach gurgled as they packed up, and she said, "Glad we're almost done here. I'm starving."

"Me too," Clayton replied, "I haven't eaten yet. Let's grab a bite to eat before we dive too far into everything."

"Sounds good to me. Where do you want to eat?" Stone asked.

"How about our usual spot?" Clayton asked.

"Sounds good to me. I'll meet ya there," Stone said as the two split up to go to their cars.

Fifteen minutes later, both cars pulled into the parking lot of the Old Mill in the heart of Lexington. The Old Mill was aptly named because, in its heyday at the turn of the century, it was a massive working mill made of huge timbers and granite. The mill worked twenty-four hours a day, turning raw cotton into cloth, mattress covers, and other bedding materials.

Now, the Old Mill has been re-purposed into different types of stores, shops, and restaurants, including a local favorite, Creekside Restaurant.

Now back together again, the two detectives walked up the sidewalk towards the restaurant's double doors. An older couple was walking out of the restaurant as they walked up. Before the detectives even got inside, they could smell the inviting smell of bacon cooking, among other breakfast foods.

As soon as the two detectives walked into the small yet ample waiting area, they heard one of the waitresses say, "Hey, ya'll," in a cheerful and friendly voice, "Is it just you two today?"

"Just us," Stone said, smiling back.

As the waitress took the two detectives to their usual booth, she asked, "Do you both want the usual to drink?"

"That's fine with us," Clayton said as they slid into the long booth.

"I'll be right back with your coffees," the waitress said, smiling.

"Thank you," Clayton said as he watched the young waitress walk away."

"She's too young for you," Stone said with a giggle, "hell, she's probably younger than I am."

"Yeah, but a guy can dream," Clayton chuckled.

"Anyway, back to the case." Stone smirked, "What do you suppose we do if the boat's registration comes up as a dead end?"

"Well, in that case, hopefully, the victim's fingerprints will be in the system somewhere, and we can get a lead that way. If not ... I don't know what we'll do."

"It would be a long shot and hopefully a last resort, but if all else fails, we could use satellite photos of the lake and plot out where the docks are and go one by one until we found something," Stone said.

"Yeah, but you're talking about hundreds of docks," Clayton said, "that would be like looking for a needle in a haystack and most definitely a last resort."

Just as Stone was starting to say something, the waitress returned with their two coffees and asked, "You two ready to order?"

"I don't know about him, but I am," Stone replied, "I'll have the ham and cheese omelet with hash browns."

"Make that two of them," Clayton replied, smiling at the young waitress.

"Not a problem. I'll be back shortly," the waitress replied warmly before turning and walking off.

After the waitress walked off, the two sat there for a couple of minutes talking about the crime scene they had just left when they spotted Kirt, the owner, walking over.

"Morning," he said cheerfully, wiping his hands on the apron wrapped around his waist, "it's been a while. Hope work's not keeping you too busy."

"Let's just say it's been a busy morning, and we're just now getting a chance to eat breakfast."

"Well, you know we can take care of that for you," Kirt said, smiling.

"That we do, my friend," Clayton replied.

"Well, I just wanted to come out and speak. Let me go back to the kitchen and see about your orders," Kirt said before rapidly walking off.

Stone was silent momentarily after Kirt walked off, and Clayton said, "I see the wheels turning. You thinking about the case already?"

"Kinda, it's something the coroner said before you got there. She said her mentor had a similar case that was never solved."

"That could be worth looking into," Clayton replied as the waitress returned with their orders.

"Can I get you anything else?" The always attentive waitress asked.

"I think we're good," Stone said with a smile.

After taking a bite of his omelet, Clayton said, "Okay, here's the plan. Let's finish eating breakfast, then we'll check on the registration for the boat. After that, we'll check in with the coroner to see what she's found so far."

"Sounds good to me," Stone said as she dug into her steaming hot omelet.

∾

AFTER THE PAIR finished eating breakfast, Stone and Clayton slowly walked into the parking lot to their cars. Before splitting up to go to their cars, Clayton said he would put in a call to SCDNR on the way back to their office to see if they could track down the owners of the boat where the victim was found.

"Sounds like a plan," Stone replied, "meet ya back at the office."

Fifteen minutes after pulling out of Creekside's parking lot, both detectives pulled up in the parking lot of the Sheriff's Department. As they walked in together, Detective Stone asked, "Were you able to make the call to SCDNR?"

"Yeah, I got them, and they told me it would take a few minutes for them to look it up. They are going to call as soon as they have a name for me," Clayton replied as the two walked inside.

After settling down at their respective desks for a few minutes, the phone on Clayton's desk rang. Amy Stone watched intently as Clayton answered the phone and said, "This is Detective Clayton." Stone listened to Clayton's side of the conversation, and judging from the way he was talking, she could tell it was SCDNR returning his call about the owner of the boat where the victim was found.

Stone watched as Clayton wrote down the information on a notepad, thanked the person on the phone, and hung up. Clayton looked at Stone, cracked a smile, and said, "Well, we have a starting point, at least."

"And just where might that be?" Stone asked.

"It's a residential neighborhood in Lexington," Clayton replied.

Instinctively, Stone grabbed her trusty notebook and said, "I think we need to go have a chat with somebody."

"That is exactly what I was thinking," Clayton said, "although this does not give me a warm and fuzzy feeling."

"What do you mean?"

"I'm not sure exactly. It just can't be this easy. It's never this easy."

"What are you talking about?" Stone asked.

"I just find it hard to believe that the first door we knock on is going to know about what's going on ... although, on the other hand, criminals are not exactly the smartest bunch of people in the world."

"Well, hopefully, we'll get lucky, and we can clear a case on the first day we get it," Stone said.

Clayton paused momentarily, smirked, and said, "That's cute."

"What's cute?"

"That you think we can clear a case the same day we get it. Haven't I taught you anything?"

"What are you talking about? Stone asked.

"It's never that easy. There's always a catch or a wrinkle," Clayton shot back.

"Not necessarily," Stone replied with a grin. "Come on, old man, I'll drive."

## 2

Twenty minutes later, the pair pulled into the driveway of a small, well-manicured house on a quiet street in the middle of Lexington. Before they even got out of the car, Clayton said, "See, what did I tell you? It was too easy. There's no sign of a boat, trailer, or anything capable of pulling a boat around here."

"For all you know, there could be something in the backyard. Don't be so pessimistic," Stone said as they got out of the car and started walking up the sidewalk.

"We'll see in a few minutes," Clayton said.

Clayton and Stone walked up the steps and rang the doorbell. It took a few moments, but they heard footsteps from inside the house slowly approaching the front door. Finally, the door opened, and the two detectives were greeted warmly by an older lady whom Stone guessed was in her mid-seventies.

"Hello. Can I help you two?" the elderly lady asked.

Stone smiled warmly, showing the lady her badge, and said, "Hello, ma'am. I'm Detective Amy Stone with the Lexington County Sheriff's Office, and this is my partner, Detective Drew Clayton. Can we ask you a few questions?"

"I don't know what I can do to help the police, but sure, you can ask anything you like. My name is Clair ... Clair Hopkins. Please come in and have a seat anywhere you like. Can I get either of you something to drink? Sweet tea, perhaps?"

"No, thank you, ma'am," Clayton said with a smile, "The reason we're here is because we are working on a case involving a boat. Do you own a boat?"

"Me? Heavens, no, but my husband Tom used to have a boat before he passed away three years ago."

"I'm sorry to hear about your husband," Stone said empathetically, "but do you know what happened to your husband's boat?"

"Not really. All I can tell you is he sold it a couple of years before he passed away, so I'd imagine it's been gone about ... five years or so."

"Ok," Stone said as she wrote everything down. "Do you know if you happen to have any paperwork around for the sale of the boat?"

"I'm afraid I don't. I needed some extra space, so my daughters came over one day and cleared out Tom's old stuff. I only saved a few mementos from his time in the service and things like photos and such."

"I see," Clayton said, "well, do you happen to remember anything about the sale of the boat, like who the boat was sold to or what the man looked like?"

"No, I'm afraid not. I just remember Tom hooked up the trailer with the boat on it and met the man in some parking lot to make the sale. I never laid eyes on him."

Stone said, "I see. Well, thank you for talking to us, and we'll let you get back to what you were doing."

"No trouble at all. I was glad to have some company. Even if it was just for a few minutes, I'm sorry I couldn't help you more than that."

"It's quite all right." Clayton again thanked the elderly lady for her time, and the two walked back to their car.

No sooner had they closed the doors then Clayton winked and said, "What did I tell you? It's never that easy."

"Yeah, yeah," Stone said with a smirk. "So, now, what do we do?"

As they backed out of the driveway, Clayton said, "Now we see about identifying the victim. Maybe, just maybe, the coroner will be finished with the preliminary report, but I kinda doubt it."

"That was my thinking as well," Stone said, "well, at least we can stop by and see if the coroner can tell us if the victim has been identified or not. Hopefully, they will have at least done fingerprints or checked dental records by now."

Not long after talking with Mrs. Hopkins about her late husband's boat, the two detectives pulled up at the Lexington County Coroner's Office not far away from their office. As the two walked inside, the secretary greeted them warmly, who instinctively picked up the phone and said, "Detectives Clayton and Stone just walked in ... I'll send them back."

As soon as she hung up the phone, the secretary said, "I'm going to buzz you in. Go on back, she's in her office."

Both detectives thanked the secretary, and Clayton pushed on the door when he heard a buzzing noise emanating from the electric latch of the door mechanism.

The pair found themselves in a small hallway. After rounding the next turn, they stopped at a door with a nameplate beside it, which simply read, Courtney King, Lexington County Coroner.

Stone took a breath and knocked.

They heard a muffled, "Door's open."

Stone opened the door, and both detectives stepped into the coroner's office, and shut the door behind them.

"Hello, you two," King said as she glanced at Stone before switching her gaze to Detective Clayton and giving him an ever-so-slight smile, "what brings you by already?"

Stone glanced at Clayton, who was holding the coroner's gaze a little too long, smirked and said, "We were hoping you could tell us if you had an ID on the victim or anything that could help us move the case forward."

"And you felt the need to drop by in person, did ya?" King replied.

Clayton replied, "Well, uh, your office is much closer than driving

all the way to the hospital, and you did tell my partner here something about this reminding you of an old case."

"True," King replied with a slight smile, "I'll give them a call and
see if they have anything for you yet, and yes, it's similar to the only
case my mentor was never able to close."

Clayton and Stone watched as the coroner picked up her cell
phone on the desk, switched it to the speaker, and called the morgue.

After the phone rang a couple of times, they heard a heavily
accented voice saying, "This is Dr. Singh."

"Hello, Dr. Singh. This is Coroner King. Have you had a chance to
finish the autopsy on the decedent from Lake Murray this morning?"

"Yes, I just finished, actually," Dr. Singh replied, "the cause of
death was exsanguination from a gunshot wound that pierced the
front torso, hitting the right axillary artery, nearly cutting it in half. I
was able to remove the bullet and sent it to SLED for further exam-
ination."

"Very well, Dr. Singh. Have you made any headway into identifying the victim?"

"Unfortunately, no, I have taken fingerprints and dental records
with no results."

"Well, that's not good," Clayton said dejectedly. "Is there anything
useful you can tell us?"

Singh paused momentarily and said, "I don't know how useful it
will be, but the bullet is slightly different than the usual types we see.
I've never seen anything quite like it before."

"What do you mean?" Clayton asked.

Singh cleared his throat and said, "The bullet I pulled from the
decedent was, for the most part, intact and weighed in at one
hundred and two grains, which is roughly the normal weight of a .380
pistol round used for self-defense."

"I sense a but coming," King said.

"And you'd be correct," Singh replied, "—but there is something
different about this bullet. It's not a standard .380 round."

"If it's not a .380 round, then what is it?" Clayton asked.

"I have no idea," Singh replied. "SLED should be able to shed some light on exactly what type of bullet it is, but it's unusual, to say the least."

About that time, King, who had been listening intently to the exchange between the detectives and Dr. Singh, piped in and asked, "Dr. Singh, did you happen to photograph the bullet?"

"Certainly," Singh replied.

King replied, "When we hang up, can you send it to me so I can have a look?"

"I would be glad to do it," Singh replied, "Will there be anything else?"

"Actually, there will. Can you please email me a copy of the report? I'd like to have a look at your findings."

Singh asked quizzically, "Dr. King, have you seen this before?"

King paused momentarily before answering and said, "Personally, no, I have not, but it's possible my mentor had."

"Really? Would you care to elaborate?" Singh asked.

"Not just yet. Let me take a look at the report. I don't want to jump to any conclusions."

"Yes, ma'am," Singh replied before hanging up.

After the call went dead and Clayton saw King check to ensure her phone was off, Clayton asked, "Well ... what's going on? What were you talking about?"

"It's nothing more than a hunch, really. The chances of this being *the* gun are ... astronomically small."

Clayton held up a hand and said, "Stop ... start from the beginning. Have you seen or heard of this gun before today?"

King took a deep breath and said, "I'm not sure, really, but my mentor was a brilliant man named Dr. John McMillian, and as I said, he had one case that he was never able to solve. When I took over the job from him, he made me promise to keep looking into it and never let it be put into a cold case drawer and be forgotten. I run the ballistics every so often to see if the gun ever turned up, but so far, nothing."

Before Clayton or Stone could ask anything else, King's computer dinged, indicating she had just gotten an email. With a few taps of her mouse, King pulled up the report of Dr. Singh's autopsy on the decedent and studied it for a few moments. Suddenly, King said, "Well, I have Singh's photo of the bullet and the autopsy report."

"So, you have seen this before," Stone said.

"As I said, personally, no, but after looking at these autopsy reports, it's at least possible that my mentor did," King said.

"Can you tell us anything about it?" Clayton asked.

"I can do ya one better than that," King said as she quickly hopped up and walked over to a filing cabinet where she opened the top drawer and rummaged through the files for a moment until the detectives heard King say, "Ah ha! Found you!"

King closed the cabinet, set the old, well-worn, and dusty file on her desk, and said, "Have a look."

Clayton reached over, opened the file, and said, "1990, Damn. Who's Jonathon Blackwood?"

"He was a gentleman who was unfortunately murdered in the spring of 1990 by a single gunshot with a unique bullet. At the time, ballistics couldn't pinpoint what type of weapon it was, but ballistics have come a long way in the past thirty-three years. Maybe now they can."

"You don't say," Clayton replied, taking in every word on the old report.

"I do say, and the kicker is, Mr. Blackwood was found floating in a boat on Lake Murray ... just like your decedent."

Both detectives looked at each other, and Stone said, shocked, "You have got to be kidding me! That can't be a coincidence!"

"Wait a minute now, let's not get ahead of ourselves," Clayton said, "the possibility that these two murders that are thirty-three years apart are linked are ... astronomical, to say the least."

"Agreed," Stone said, "I think it'd be best if we just wait for the SLED report on the ballistics. That will hopefully tell us for sure whether it's the same gun or not, and if it is—"

Clayton interrupted Stone, saying, "If it is, we may close two cases simultaneously."

"Exactly, and I can retire into the sunset knowing I helped to close my mentor's case for him, just like I promised," King said with a smile.

Clayton said, "Can you make me a copy of that file before we go? I want to look up our old case file on the 1990 murder and see what we have. With any luck, we'll be able to track down our old case file, and if we find it, maybe, just maybe, we'll get lucky and find something the initial investigators missed."

Clayton and Stone stood up, thanked King, and left her office. "Well, I know what we're going to be doing the rest of the afternoon," Stone said.

"I don't think you do," Clayton replied.

"So, we're not going to be looking for the old case file from 1990?" Stone said.

"I will. You, however, will be doing something else," Clayton replied.

"And just what is that exactly?"

"I want you to go back and talk to the witnesses who found the boat floating in the lake. See if they can tell you exactly where the boat was when they saw it. Hopefully, we can at least narrow down the search where the boat came from."

"And if we can do that, we can hopefully figure out where she was shot," Stone replied.

"Exactly," Clayton replied, "now you're thinking like a detective."

Stone smiled and said, "I was thinking like a detective a few minutes ago, too, when I saw you and the coroner making eyes at each other."

Clayton tried to play it off, saying, "What are you talking about?"

"You know exactly what I'm talking about. The coy smiles at each other and how you started stuttering the minute we walked into her office. From another woman's perspective, there's no doubt that she likes you."

"No, she doesn't. There's no way," Clayton said in a dismissive tone.

Giggling at seeing Clayton squirm a little, Stone smiled and said, "I'm telling you, she likes you."

Clayton smirked and said, "Drive rookie."

Stone dropped Clayton back off at the Sheriff's Office, and the pair went their separate ways for the rest of the afternoon, each with their own task for the case: Clayton to find the old case file from 1990 and Stone to reinterview the witnesses from the new case.

## 3

The following morning, the two detectives met at the Sheriff's Department to go over what they knew about the case.

"Good morning," Clayton said as he walked in with two cups of coffee.

"Good morning, and thanks for the coffee. I was hoping you didn't forget it was your turn," Stone replied.

"A cop worth his salt never forgets his partner's coffee," Clayton replied with a wink and a smile.

"So, were you able to find the 1990 case file on Jonathon Blackwood?"

"It took a while, but I did, and his murder reads very much like our current murder. I have yet to find the actual physical evidence box, but from what I can tell, he was shot and found adrift in a boat near the towers of Lake Murray one morning by a couple of fishermen. What about you? Were the people who found the boat able to help us out any?"

Stone shook her head and said, "Not much. All they could say for certain was that they found the boat adrift about a mile or so straight out from the dam."

"Well, at least both boats were found on the same end of the lake and not the opposite end of the lake," Clayton replied.

"Was there a ballistics report in the file for Jonathon Blackwood? Stone asked.

"Yes and no," Clayton replied, "the bullet was beat up pretty bad. According to the coroner's report from back then, the bullet entered Blackwood's back near the spine, nicked a lung, and hit Blackwood's heart."

"And the gun was never found?" Stone asked.

"Nope, at the time, detectives probably thought the weapon was disposed of in the lake, which is exactly what I would have done because some parts of the lake are two hundred feet deep. There's no way a gun would have ever been found if it was tossed in there."

Stone sat there for a moment and said, "So, let me get this straight: this Jonathon Blackwood character gets killed thirty-three years ago, and suddenly, someone kills a young woman with the same type of weapon? A weapon we can't identify, and both bodies are found in an eerily similar way. That can't be a coincidence. Can it?"

"I have no idea," Clayton replied, "but I know one thing."

"What's that?"

"We need to identify our victim. If we can do that, we may get a lead. Also, when the actual evidence box is found, I want to forward what little ballistics information there is in the Blackwood murder to SLED and see if they can confirm whether or not those are the same kind of bullets or not."

"It's a shot in the dark. What do we have to lose at this point?" Stone replied.

"Also, I want to see if a missing person's report has been filed within the past twenty-four hours or so. Maybe we can find a match that way." Clayton said.

"I'll see what I can come up with," Stone replied as she picked up the phone on her desk and started dialing.

"And while you do that ... I'll check with SLED to see if they have had a chance to check ballistics on our bullet from yesterday," Clayton replied, "maybe we'll get lucky."

"We need a little bit of luck right now, that's for sure," Stone replied.

"Tell me about it," Clayton shot back as he picked up the phone to call SLED.

After being transferred to their firearms department, the phone rang a few times before Clayton heard someone say, "Ballistics, Detective Wilson speaking."

"Detective Wilson, this is Detective Drew Clayton with the Lexington County Sheriff's Office. I was hoping you were able to complete a ballistics report on the bullet from my crime scene yesterday."

"Yeah, I did. You have quite the find, that's for sure. Where did this bullet come from?"

"That's the million-dollar question, I'm afraid," Clayton said, "That particular bullet came out of a victim found in a boat on Lake Murray. Why?"

"Because I can't say exactly what type of weapon fired that bullet, but I can tell you that it was not one of ours."

"What do you mean when you say it's not one of ours?" Clayton asked.

"What I mean is that it's definitely not from around here," Wilson replied.

"Can you be more specific?"

"If I were to guess ... I'd say you were looking at some sort of antique weapon."

Shocked, Clayton asked, "What kind of antique, and do you have a guess as to how old the weapon could be?"

Wilson chuckled at Clayton's response and said, "It's likely a pistol round, and for age, I can only guess early turn of the century ... possibly World War II. It's definitely not an American-made weapon. The closest thing we have to this bullet is a .32, but it's not a .32 at all."

Clayton asked, "Any guesses as to what country it came from, and if it's not a .32 but close, what is it?"

"Believe it or not, it's an actual 8mm round, and another thing is the ammo is quite old."

"How can you tell?" Clayton asked.

"Old ammunition just has a different look under a microscope compared to a new round."

"I see," Clayton replied, "well, let's say, hypothetically, if I get you another bullet like the one we're talking about, can you tell me if it were fired from the same gun?"

"As long as the bullet is in good shape ... sure it's possible," Wilson replied.

"Okay, thank you. I'll be in touch," Clayton replied before hanging up.

As soon as Clayton hung up the phone, Stone looked at him and asked, "Well, what did you find out?"

"You're not going to believe this shit," Clayton replied.

"What is it?" Stone asked.

"That bullet comes from some kind of antique," Clayton replied.

"Antique as in a hundred years old, antique?"

"Believe it or not ... yes," Clayton shot back.

"Could it have been some vets bring back or war trophy?"

"I guess anything's possible. That could explain why it's a rarity around here." Clayton replied, "I'm just stumped with the weapon for now."

"It's not your typical murder weapon, for sure. That puts a twist in the case, and it could explain why the gun wasn't tossed after the first murder ... sentimental reasons."

"Well, if it weren't tossed after the first murder, I'd say most likely the gun is now sitting on the bottom of the lake, that's for sure," Clayton said.

"Yes, indeed, especially if the same gun was used in both murders," Stone replied.

"I gotta call the property clerk and get them working on finding that evidence box," Clayton replied, "We gotta find that bullet from the Blackwood murder. Did you get anything from missing persons?"

"No, nothing yet," Stone replied dejectedly.

Clayton picked up the phone and dialed the number for the property clerk. After telling the clerk who he was and what he was looking for, the clerk referred him to the property warehouse across town.

Clayton promptly thanked the clerk, hung up for a split second, then he dialed a new number. Stone listened intently to Clayton's side of the conversation, and before Clayton hung up the phone, she knew there was a problem.

"What is it?" Stone asked.

"That was the property clerk at the warehouse where the older case files and unsolved murder property boxes go. He told me several more recent cases ahead of ours needed his attention, but he would call me back as soon as he could get to it. He said it would hopefully be in about an hour or so."

"Are you sure this isn't a wild goose chase?" Stone asked.

"No, not really. It could be a strange coincidence, but the coroner's report is compelling, to say the least, and King seemed to believe it. That's good enough for me to at least look into the possibility of the two murders being connected."

A LITTLE OVER AN HOUR LATER, the two detectives pulled up at the secure property warehouse where the older evidence was kept. As they hopped out, Clayton asked, "Have you ever been here before?"

"Nope, can't say that I have," Stone replied, "but until now, I haven't needed to come over here."

"Well, you're in for a real treat. Be prepared to get your hands dirty. Some of these boxes haven't been touched in over a decade," Clayton shot back.

"Oh, lovely," Stone replied, rolling her eyes.

The two detectives walked inside and found that they were standing in a small waiting room. As the two entered, they saw an older man with all-white hair look up from behind the counter. The man behind the counter stood up, opened the small bank-teller-style window, and in a gruff voice said, "What case are you here looking for?"

As soon as Clayton laid eyes on the older man, he smiled and said, "Well, I'll be damned if it isn't Jack O'Neal. I thought they had put you out to pasture years ago!"

The old man took a hard look at the older detective and said, "Drew, is that you?"

"Sure is," Clayton replied with a smile, "Why in the hell are you still working? You were old as dirt when we were detectives together."

"Keeps me busy; besides, the Mrs. appreciates me not being home so much," O'Neal giggled, "So what can I do for you?"

"First off, this is my new partner, Amy Stone. She just made detective last year and—"

Before Clayton could finish his sentence, O'Neal giggled and said, "And they stuck you with this old fossil? Who did you piss off? Nah, really, you could do much worse. Listen to everything he tells you, and you'll do fine."

"I've learned a lot already," Stone replied with a smile as she enjoyed seeing the banter between the two old friends.

"We picked up a new case yesterday morning, and it's a long shot, but it may have something to do with a case from 1990."

"Was it you that called about the Blackwood evidence box?"

"Yep, it was me," Clayton replied.

O'Neal asked, "And you think your new case may be connected to the Blackwood case?"

Clayton replied, "Not yet, but the coroner thought the murders were similar enough to tell us about the theory, and I must say they're similar. Both were found shot and floating on a boat out in Lake Murray. For the current coroner's mentor, the 1990 case was the one that kept him up at night, so our current corner vowed to keep looking when he retired. Now, when this case came up, she recognized the similarities. Why? Do you know anything about the Blackwood murder?"

"Not really. I wasn't a part of the investigation. Still, there were rumors of Blackwood being part of a business deal for a plot of land on the lake with one of the Harrington boys, but after he was found dead and then Blackwood murdered, nothing more ever happened about it that I can remember anyway. Wish I could help ya more."

Clayton and Stone glanced at each other, and Clayton asked, "Wait, you mean *the* Harringtons? As in one of the wealthiest families around here, Harringtons? How is it that I haven't heard about this other death before now?"

"Yeah, that's the family, but there wasn't anything to it," O'Neal replied as he rubbed his chin. "Seems like the Harrington kid was the black sheep of the family, and he was found dead, but I don't remember how exactly. Seems like it was ruled an accident or something. We looked, but no connection was ever made between the two deaths, and the Harrington case quietly went away."

Stone asked, "Was the Harrington death covered up, ya think?"

O'Neal rubbed his chin momentarily and said, "Can't say for certain. Like I said, I wasn't on the case, but as I remember, it simply went away. You want to have a look at the Blackwood evidence box?"

"Sure do!" Clayton said excitedly.

"Sign the log with all the information, and I'll unlock the door and bring you two back so you can have a look."

After both detectives signed the logbook, O'Neal unlocked the door and escorted them to a small room with a table in the middle, giving them enough room to walk around comfortably.

"Hang tight, and I'll be right back," O'Neal said as he left the room. Moments later, he returned with a cardboard box usually reserved for old files, sat the box on the table, and said, "Here ya go. I am required to tell you that you are being monitored," as he pointed to the camera with a flashing light on top.

"Not a problem," Clayton replied.

"I'll leave you two with it," O'Neal said as he turned and walked out.

Clayton took a deep breath and said, "Here we go," as he unsealed the box for the first time in nearly thirty years and looked inside.

"Everything looks pretty good," Stone said.

"Yep, that's good," Clayton replied, "let's see what we have."

Before they reached into the box and touched anything, both

detectives put on a pair of rubber gloves they that always kept handy. After situating the gloves like he wanted, Clayton reached in and took out several individually sealed bags that were in the box.

Once he emptied the box, Clayton sat it on the floor to give them room to spread out the contents of the evidence box on the table. After spreading the bags out, the first thing they saw was a light tan colored shirt that had deep, dark burgundy stains all over, which, due to the passage of time, were almost black. The pants he was wearing were also in the evidence box, which also had the same visible deep, dark stains.

Yet another smaller evidence bag, which was labeled, one wallet with contents. Along with the wallet, the contents of the wallet were also indicated on the evidence bag.

"Geez, look at all the blood stains on his clothes. No wonder he didn't make it," Stone said, "He must have bled out just like our victim."

"Probably so," Clayton replied as he shuffled through the different evidence bags. After a moment of searching, Clayton huffed and said, "We have a problem."

"What's that?" Stone asked as she looked through the evidence bags.

"There's no bullet," Clayton replied.

"Shouldn't it be here with the physical evidence?" Stone asked.

"It should be," Clayton replied as he again picked up the evidence storage box and read the evidence label on the outside of it.

Stone listened intently as Clayton read off the contents that were supposed to be in the evidence box. As Clayton called out the number for each piece of evidence, Stone found the number on the table and made a mental note that it was there.

Now, getting down toward the short list of evidence that was supposed to be in the box, Clayton read off a number and said, "One bag containing one bullet. Shit! It's not here."

"It's gotta be here. It's listed in the evidence box," Stone shot back.

"Let's go over everything again before I get O'Neal back in here," Clayton replied dejectedly.

As the two went over every piece of evidence again that was in the box, Clayton picked up the box and dropped it on the table. When he did, they both heard something rolling around inside the box.

Clayton and Stone looked inside to see that one of the flaps had moved upward slightly when Clayton dropped the box, and now the missing bullet was sitting in plain sight.

Clayton excitedly said, "The bullet must have somehow gotten under the flap, and when I dropped it on the table just now, it popped out!"

Smiling from ear to ear, Stone said, "I sure am glad you found that bullet. Maybe now we can find out once and for all if these two cases are connected."

"Exactly," Clayton replied, "we need to get O'Neal back in here because we have some paperwork to complete."

Once Clayton and Stone got O'Neal involved and the appropriate paperwork was completed, they signed the bullet out of evidence, thanked O'Neal for the helping hand, and started for the door.

As the two detectives started out, Clayton turned and asked, "Say, O'Neal, do you remember the name of the other person who died you were telling us about?"

"The other person's name was Harrington for sure ... I think his first name was Peter, but I could be wrong. It was a long time ago, after all."

The two detectives thanked O'Neal again and went straight to SLED to drop off the bullet.

ON THEIR WAY over to the ballistics lab at SLED, as she drove, Stone glanced over at Clayton in the passenger's seat and asked, "You're quiet. What's up?"

"Just thinking about the case and what's going to happen if we find out that the same gun fired these two bullets," Clayton replied.

"Was the Harrington family powerful enough to make the investigation disappear?" Stone asked.

"Honestly, I don't know, but by today's standards, it seems shady at best, but we shouldn't get ahead of ourselves just yet. It's a real longshot that these deaths are connected."

"True," Stone conceded. The rest of the ride over to SLED was quiet, with each detective lost in their own thoughts about the case on the drive over to Broad River Road.

Before long, Stone pulled into the parking lot at SLED, and they walked inside to find Detective Wilson. As they stood inside conferring with Wilson, Stone's cell phone started to ring. She took a few steps away from Wilson and Clayton to hear what was being said. Clayton glanced over at Stone in time to see her eyes widen and hear her say, "We'll be right there, thanks."

As Stone walked over to where Clayton and Wilson were standing, Clayton asked, "What was that about?"

Stone said, "We gotta go."

"Why? What's up?" Clayton asked.

Stone replied, "A woman came into the Sheriff's Department and filled out a missing person report. She also brought in a picture of her missing daughter. Guess who the description seems to match up with? The description had the same hair and eye color, petite frame, and the cross tattoo on her wrist."

Clayton looked at Wilson and asked, "Will you give me a call as soon as you know something?"

"Be glad to do it," Wilson replied.

The three shook hands, and as Clayton and Stone left, Clayton said, "This could be the break we've been needing."

"Yeah, and get this; I didn't want to say it in front of Wilson, but guess what the person's name was that came in and filled the report out."

"I can already tell this is going to be bad. Who is it?"

"The person who came in to make the report was the mother of the missing girl. The missing girl's name is Anna Blackwood."

Clayton's eyes widened, and he replied with shock, "Blackwood, as in Jonathon Blackwood, who was murdered in 1990 ... that Blackwood?"

"Apparently so," Stone said.

Clayton took a deep breath and said, "I knew I should have retired last year. We need to swing by the station, pull up the name on the missing person report, and have a look at the picture. I want to see if we can get a DMV hit with the name. If so, and we can match it to the picture of the missing girl ... we'll know."

Once back at their office, the two detectives quickly walked to their side-by-side desks, and Stone watched while Clayton pulled up the missing person report taken earlier in the day. Taking the name from the missing person report, Clayton entered it into a different database, complete with DMV photos, and within moments, the two detectives were looking at a DMV photo of their victim.

"It sure looks like our victim," Stone replied.

"That it does. I'm going to forward everything over to Dr. Singh. Then I'm going to call him to see if he can positively identify that this is the same girl that's lying in his morgue." Clayton replied.

After he forwarded the tentative identification and photographs, Clayton put the phone on speaker and called the Lexington County Coroner, Courtney King.

On the second ring, Clayton heard King pick up, and as usual, she said, "This is Courtney."

As soon as Stone heard the coroner's voice through the speaker, she smirked at Clayton, who was trying in vain not to pay attention to her. "This is Detective Clayton at the Sheriff's office. Um, I just sent some photos over to Dr. Singh and wanted to know if he could identify the young woman in the morgue. I'd call him directly, but I didn't know his direct line."

King replied in a flirtatious manner, "You mean you're a detective, and you couldn't find Dr. Singh's number?"

Clayton's cheeks flushed as he noticed Stone watching and smiling at him stumble over his words. Clayton picked up the receiver and said, "I could have, but I figured this was faster."

Stone listened to Clayton's end of the conversation for a few moments, then he wrote a number on a sticky note, thanked King, and hung up the phone. Before he had a chance to dial the number, Stone asked, smiling, "When are you going to ask her out?"

Ignoring the question, Clayton dialed the number King had given him, and this time, he put the call back on speaker. After a couple of rings, both detectives heard the thick accent of Dr. Singh answer the phone.

"Dr Singh, this is Detective Clayton, and you're on speaker with Detective Amy Stone. I've sent you a DMV photograph and a missing persons report. I'd like you to have a look and see if this is the same person lying in your morgue."

"Give me five minutes, and I will look at my findings. I will call you back shortly." Singh replied.

Clayton gave Singh his direct number, and as soon as he put the phone down, Stone asked, "Well?"

"Well, what?" Clayton replied.

"When are you going to ask her out?"

"I'm not," Clayton replied, "Listen, kid, I'm an old and worn-out detective. I just want to finish my last year so I can go fishing every weekend in peace and quiet. Besides, she wouldn't be interested in me."

"Are you kidding me? Did you hear how she was flirting with you on the phone just a minute ago?" She's interested," Stone said, trying to talk some sense into Clayton.

Before he could respond, Clayton's phone rang, and he immediately picked it up and put it on speaker, "Clayton here," he replied, skipping the formalities.

"This is Dr. Singh, and I have some news for you."

"What kind of news do you have?" Clayton replied as he bobbed his head from side to side as some people from India do. While they waited for a response from Singh, Stone had to turn her head to keep from laughing aloud at Clayton.

Singh said, "After reviewing the details of your missing person report, including the photograph, the DMV photo you provided, and my own findings ... I can say with certainty that the unidentified person is, in fact, Anna Blackwood. I want to stress that I have no known DNA samples of Miss Blackwood to compare, but I feel certain that these two people are one and the same. If you can get me a toothbrush known to have been Anna Blackwood's, we'll be able to say one hundred percent whether it's the same person."

Before hanging up the phone, Stone asked, "How sure are you now, Dr. Singh, without the DNA to back up your findings?"

Singh thought for a moment and said, "I am ninety percent certain that this is the same person. There is always a chance that it's not, but in this instance ... I don't think so."

Both detectives thanked Dr. Singh, and Clayton hung up the phone and said, "Now, you know the next step."

"Yep, Notification," Stone said somberly.

# 4

The ride over to the address given to Stone was quiet and somber because both had a bad feeling they were about to break a family's spirit. "You ready for this?" Clayton asked.

"Not really, but it's not the first time I've done a notification," Stone said as she thought back to the time when she had to make a notification after a car crash. It took her months to get the sound of the mother's wailing out of her head after a drunk driver killed her son.

"Yeah, I know, but it never gets any easier," Clayton said somberly as they exited the car and started up the front sidewalk.

Clayton and Stone stepped up onto the front porch of the relatively new home and rang the doorbell. The front door opened momentarily, and the two detectives saw a middle-aged woman who was visibly upset and had obviously been crying recently.

Noticing their badges immediately, the somber woman asked, "Have you found her?"

Ignoring the question momentarily, Clayton said, "Ma'am, I'm Detective Drew Clayton, and this is my partner, Detective Amy Stone. Can we come in and talk about a missing person report you filed?"

"Yes, of course," the woman replied somberly.

Clayton and Stone followed the woman into the living room, where they found an older couple with their arms around each other, obviously deeply concerned about their missing family member. The tension in the air was already high, but it seemed to magnify ten-fold when the two detectives walked in.

The older man stood up and said, "I'm ... I'm Nathan Blackwood. This is my wife Melissa and my daughter Anabelle ... Have you found my granddaughter?"

Clayton looked at Annabelle and asked, "So, Anna is your daughter, correct?"

"Yes, that's correct," Annabelle replied with a trembling voice.

Stone asked, "Ma'am, do you have a picture of your daughter?"

"Why? You've found someone, haven't you?" Anabelle asked as her voice cracked.

Stone could tell that Clayton obviously didn't want to say what he needed to say, but finally, Clayton took a deep breath and said, "Ma'am, yesterday morning, we were called to a scene where a person was found ... deceased."

With a horrified look on her face, Anabelle nearly screamed, "DID YOU FIND MY DAUGHTER DEAD? IS MY DAUGHTER DEAD?"

Tears were streaming down Nathan Blackwood's face, and Melissa began to cry openly as Clayton said, "I'm so sorry, but what we know is the victim ... matches the description you gave the police earlier. There was no identification on the victim, and we were not sure until you filed the missing person report. Using the name you provided, we were able to pull up Anna's DMV record and make a tentative identification."

"Is it her? What about her wrist? Was there a cross tattoo there?

Well, is it my granddaughter or not?" Nathan asked with a trembling voice.

Clayton said, "It will be up to the coroner to make the final determination, but the victim ... appears to be Anna."

The words hit Anabelle like a run-away locomotive as she struggled to keep her feet under her. Thinking quickly, Stone wrapped her arms around the grieving mother and guided her to the couch beside her parents, where all three hugged and cried like babies.

After a few moments, Clayton said, "I want to stress that there is a chance that this is not your daughter. Again, it will be up to the coroner."

After trying to gather himself together, Nathan Blackwood asked, "When ... when will the coroner know for sure?"

"As soon as we can compare DNA to something Anna was known to use, such as a toothbrush, we'll be able to say one hundred percent."

Trying to latch on to the tiniest bit of hope, Anabelle's mother, Melissa, said, "So, does that mean they're not sure?"

Clayton took a breath, looked at the ceiling, and said, "I'm sorry to say they are sure it is Anna. The DNA would just be used to confirm that it is Anna."

Annabelle's mother wrapped her arms around Annabelle and held her tightly as all three sat on the couch, sobbing uncontrollably for the next ten minutes.

"Can I do anything for you? Put on a pot of coffee for you, perhaps?" Stone asked.

In between his daughters' wails, the elder Blackwood wiped his tears, stood, and said, "I'll help. I know where everything is." As Nathan hopped up, Melissa wrapped her arms around their daughter and openly cried with her.

As they walked into the kitchen, Nathan said somberly, "Thank you for giving us hope, detective, but obviously, you feel as if it's our Anna, or you would not be here."

As the Keurig heated up, Stone asked, "Do you know anything about her life, like what she may have been doing or what kind of work she did?"

Nathan thought for a moment and said, "I know she was into writing and was writing a book, but I don't know what it was about. I know she kept tight-lipped about it. Anna might know, though."

Several minutes later, after they had made a cup of coffee for each of the Blackwood family members, Stone and Nathan cautiously walked back into the living room with the steaming hot liquid.

When they returned with the coffee cups, Stone asked Anna, "Mrs. Blackwood, can you give us any information about what your daughter did for a living?"

In between crying spells and wiping her tears, Annabelle sniffled and glanced at her dad rather uncomfortably for a moment, then said, "I know she was writing a book, but she ... she wouldn't say what it was."

"I see," Stone replied, "Ma'am, did your daughter live here with you?"

"No, she had an apartment a few miles from here, further into Lexington on Lake Murray Boulevard. Why?"

"When was the last time you went over there?" Stone asked.

"I went yesterday afternoon when I realized I hadn't talked to Anna lately and went over to check on her."

"And how did the apartment look inside?" Clayton asked.

"In a word, immaculate," Anabelle replied, "she liked everything in its place."

Stone asked, "Would you mind letting us go to Anna's apartment to look around?"

"Not at all. Let me get you a key," Anabelle replied as she wiped tears off her cheeks.

Moments later, Anabelle returned with a key and handed it to Stone along with a piece of paper with the address of Anna's apartment, saying, "Look all you like. Just make sure we get the key back when you're done."

"We can do that, and thank you," Stone replied.

"What are you hoping to find?" Anabelle asked.

"Well, for one thing, we're going to retrieve her toothbrush, so we can positively say yes, this is Anna. After that, we will look around to see what we can see. We could obtain a court order if that would make you feel more comfortable about the situation, but that would take time."

"No, by all means, do what you must," Anabelle replied somberly.

Slowly, Nathan walked the two detectives to the front door and said, "If it turns out to be Anna, find out who did this to her."

Clayton shook Nathans's hand and replied, "We fully intend to. We'll keep you posted on what we find."

No sooner had the two detectives gotten in their car and started out of the driveway when Clayton asked, "Did you see how Anabelle glanced at her dad before saying what she did about the book?"

"Yeah, I noticed it too. It's as if she knew but didn't want to say in front of her father what the book was about."

"I got that vibe also," Clayton replied, "With any luck, we can find some research materials in Anna's apartment."

"That's a definite possibility because if not, we are going to have to get Anabelle alone and ask her what she knows about the book," Stone said.

NOT LONG AFTER leaving Anabelle Blackwood's home, the two detectives pulled into a small set of apartments on Bush River Road, less than a mile from the lake.

Within a few moments of pulling off the main road, they found Anna's apartment number, parked, and walked up to the front door.

Purely on instinct, Clayton reached out and knocked on the door. "You know, if somebody opens that door, I'm going to have a stroke. Right?" Stone said with a smirk.

Chuckling, Clayton replied, "Yeah, but it would be funny for a second or two."

Stone playfully smacked Clayton on the arm with the back of her hand and said, "I'm going to open it with the key we got from the victim's mother."

Clayton watched as Stone pulled out the key Anabelle Blackwood had given them earlier and had to forcefully push the key into the lock. The door came open as soon as Stone pushed the key into the lock. Instantly, both detectives saw the tool marks and realized the door had been forced at some point.

Both detectives drew their service weapons, called for backup, and cautiously entered the apartment, saying aloud, "Lexington County Sheriff's Office! Is there anyone in here?"

"Clear right," Clayton said in a low tone as he entered.

"Clear left," Stone replied as she quickly followed him in.

The two detectives pushed further into the small apartment, clearing the bathroom and bedroom without incident.

"Look at this place. It's been wrecked," Stone said, shocked.

Both detectives stood in the living room of the one-bedroom apartment and looked around, noting that the couch cushions had been tossed about and all the drawers had been opened and rummaged through.

"Okay, what in the hell is going on here?" Clayton asked as he examined the area in disbelief. Moments later, they heard the unmistakable sound of sirens closing in on their location.

Shortly, the small apartment complex was filled with flashing lights and curious onlookers as police descended on the area. After ensuring the area of Anna's apartment was secure, detectives procured a toothbrush from Anna's bathroom for a DNA sample.

Once that was complete, Stone called to tell Anabelle Blackwood about what they found when they arrived, and it would be very beneficial if she would come over to do a walk-through of the apartment and see if she could tell what, if anything, was missing.

While they waited for Anabelle Blackwood to show up, the detectives went to the apartment next door to Anna's to determine wheather they heard or saw anything. As they walked over, an older man sat on the adjacent apartment's stoop and asked, "What's going on? Is Anna, okay?"

After introducing themselves to the neighbor, Stone asked, "Did you hear or see anything unusual lately? Anything that may have been out of the ordinary for Miss Blackwood?"

The man rubbed his chin and said, "I haven't seen Anna in a couple of days now, but I did see some fella leaving her place last night."

"Have you seen this man before?"

"Nope, can't say that I have. Why? What's going on? Is Anna, okay?"

Could you describe him, or did you see what kind of car maybe?"

"Nope, I couldn't see him, but the car was a dark-colored newer model four-door with rental tags. Now, is Anna, okay or not?"

Ignoring the question, Clayton asked, "And you're sure it was last night when you saw this man leaving her apartment?"

"Positive," the man replied, frustrated, "Now what is going on?"

"All I can say at this time is we are working on a case," Stone replied, "thank you for your time."

The two detectives turned and walked back to Anna's apartment. Once they were out of earshot of the neighbor, Stone said, "If the neighbor is correct on his timeline, Anna was already dead when someone broke in here."

"That's what I was thinking as well. Do you think it could have anything to do with this book she was writing?"

"I don't know, but we need to find out, that's for sure," Clayton replied, come on, let's go look around the apartment."

As they entered, they looked closely at how things were moved and strewn about, especially around what seemed to be her home office or workspace. All the drawers were open and had been gone through as well. That's when they noticed that there was no laptop or computer.

"There's a cord for a laptop and something else, possibly an external hard drive," Stone said.

"It sure looks like it," Clayton replied.

"Well, whatever was here, it's gone now. Maybe the external hard drive was backed up to the cloud somewhere."

"What do you mean backed up to the cloud?" Clayton asked.

"It's too hard to explain," Stone said with a smirk.

"People just need to go back to the good ole' days of pen and paper," Clayton replied, "there was nothing wrong with that."

"Yeah, until you lose your notepad, your pen runs out of ink, or the paper gets wet and is illegible," Stone said with a giggle.

Just then, a sheriff's deputy walked in and said, "Detectives, there are three people outside looking for you. One of them is Anabelle Blackwood. She said you called her to come over."

"Here we go," Clayton said as both detectives followed the sheriff's deputy outside to where Anabelle stood.

Before either detective could say a thing, Anabelle asked, "How bad is it?"

"Thank you for coming," Clayton replied as the detectives escorted Anabelle into Anna's ransacked apartment.

Stopping at the door to the apartment, Clayton said, "Ma'am, I'm afraid I must ask you not to touch anything. The apartment is still being processed. We want to know if you see anything missing."

Shaking her head, she understood. Clayton and Stone escorted Anabelle into the apartment. Anabelle gasped at seeing the once neat apartment, and tears ran down her cheeks.

"Ma'am, are you all right?" Stone asked.

Taking a moment to answer, Anabelle shook her head up and down and muttered, "Yes, I'm fine."

As the three slowly walked through the apartment, Anabelle stopped at Anna's desk and workspace, noting that some items were missing.

"What's missing?" Clayton asked.

"Um, there was a laptop, an external hard drive, and a notebook she used to keep notes in. It's all gone," Anabelle asked.

"What kind of notes?" Stone asked.

"I'm not sure, really, but I assume it was notes for her book."

"And what kind of book was she writing?" Clayton asked.

Anabelle was silent for a moment, and before she could respond, Stone emphasized, "Ma'am, we know you're aware of the book. When we asked you at your house earlier, you didn't want to say in front of your parents. It could help us greatly if you tell us what she was writing about."

Anabelle took a deep breath and said, "The murder of Jonathon Blackwood."

## 5

"What do you mean she was writing a book on the Jonathon Blackwood murder?" Stone asked.

Anabelle took a deep breath and said, "There are those in the Blackwood family that have always felt as if someone in the Harrington family had something to do with Jonathon's murder. As time passed and Anna got older, she became hell-bent on figuring out who killed Jonathon, despite my father's objections."

"But you knew about it, and that's why you didn't want to say anything in front of your father."

"Yes, I knew he would be upset. He had repeatedly told Anna to stay away from the Harrington's, but she would not leave it alone."

Stone asked, "And what about Anna's father? Is he in the picture?"

"No, he's dead. He was killed in a helicopter crash on a training mission."

"What did Anna do to make money? Did she have a job?"

"She worked part-time as a waitress at night, and she also did some work as an independent journalist. You don't really think this has something to do with Jonathon Blackwood's murder, do you?"

Clayton thought for a moment and said, "It's hard to say. It could be a coincidence. Did Anna have somebody she was working on the book with, like a publisher or somebody that would have known about the details of the book?"

"Her friend Riley was an editor. I know Anna had mentioned that Riley was editing the book for her," Anabelle replied.

"Do you know where this Riley lives or her last name by chance?" Clayton asked.

"Yes, her last name is Hampton, Riley Hampton."

"Thank you, you've been a huge help," Stone said.

"Wait, what do I do about the apartment?" Anabelle asked.

"Nothing. Crime scene people will be here for a few hours dusting for fingerprints, and when that's done, they will secure the apartment. Just go back home, and one of us will call you with an update as soon as we know something. We will release the apartment back to you as soon as possible, but for now ... it's still a crime scene."

As Anabelle fought back more tears, she said, "Okay, thank you both for all you have done." After that, Anabelle turned, slowly returned to her car and drove off.

Stone looked at Clayton and said, "What is it? You have that look on your face like something's not right."

"I want to go back inside for a minute," Clayton replied.

"What for?

"I saw something in the apartment that, after talking to Anabelle now, doesn't fit."

"What are you talking about?" Stone asked as she followed Clayton back into the apartment.

Clayton initially ignored the question but walked over to where the desk was located and started looking at the papers tossed on the floor by the intruder. Squatting down by some loose papers, he saw what he was looking for, then called for the crime scene photographer to ensure he photographed them before Clayton touched anything.

After snapping several photographs of the papers from different angles, the photographer gave Clayton the thumbs up, and Clayton picked up the paper he was interested in. "It looks like a paycheck stub," Stone said.

Clayton smiled and said, "It is, but look where the stub is from."

Stone's eyes widened when she read the block lettering of HARRINGTON LLC made out to Anna Watkins.

"Who's Anna Watkins?" Stone asked.

Clayton asked, "What do you want to bet that Watkins is Anabelle Blackwood's maiden name?"

"If that's true, Anna must have used her mom's maiden name to get a job working for the Harrington's to gain insight into Jonathon Blackwood's murder."

"We need to talk to the friend, Riley Hampton, and ask her about the book and the job. Maybe she can shed more light on what Anna was looking into."

"So, you think this is all connected then?" Stone asked.

"Oh, yeah, I'm sure ... this murder, the break-in, it's all connected to a thirty-year-old unsolved murder. Anna found out something that got her killed."

"What about the DNA evidence we initially came here to get before we walked into this mess?" Stone asked.

Clayton glanced at his watch and said, "Change of plans ... It's getting late in the afternoon, so we'll have a uniformed officer take the toothbrush to the coroner's lab to maintain the chain of custody, and we'll talk to the friend. If somebody in the Harrington family is trying to cover their tracks and they figure out Miss Hampton has information on the book, she very well could be in danger."

ONCE THE TWO detectives left Anna's apartment, Stone called the office and obtained Riley Hampton's last known address, which, as it turns out, was not far away.

As the two drove over to what they hoped was Hampton's apartment, Stone said, "You don't think Anna could have really figured out who killed Jonathon Blackwood over thirty years ago. Do you?"

"Honestly, I think she stumbled onto something she shouldn't have, and that's what got her killed. I don't know what it was, but whatever it was that she found, somebody did not want it getting out. That's for sure," Clayton replied.

A few minutes later, the detectives pulled into the main entrance of a nicer-looking apartment complex. After spending the next couple of minutes driving around, they spotted the building number they were searching for. After that, it was a breeze to find the actual apartment number.

Once they found the apartment number, Stone knocked on the door. Almost at once, a young woman opened the door and said, "Wow, that was fast. I just called a few minutes ago."

Stone and Clayton looked at each other, momentarily caught off guard, and then Clayton said, "Are you Riley Hampton?"

"Yes, sir. That's me. I'm the one who called."

Stone said, "There must be some confusion. We're here because of another matter. Did you call the police for something?"

"Wait, you're not here for the break-in then?" Riley asked.

"No, ma'am, sorry," Clayton said, "What break-in?"

"Oh," Riley replied dejected, "I should have known they would not have sent two detectives for a car break-in. What did you want with me?"

Clayton said, "As my partner started to say, we're here for another matter. Do you mind if we come in for a few minutes?"

Riley stepped back, letting the two detectives into her apartment as the unsettling realization began to hit her that something was terribly wrong.

"What's going on? What's wrong?" Riley asked.

Stone replied, "Do you know Anna Blackwood?"

"Sure, I know Anna, I'm helping her with her book. Why?"

Ignoring the question at first, Stone asked, "Can you tell me about the book? What was it about?"

Riley said, "She was writing a book about the thirty-three-year-old murder of someone in her family named Jonathon Blackwood. Why?"

Again, ignoring the question momentarily, Stone asked, "Do you have a copy of that book? Can we see it?"

"Actually, that's why I called you guys," Riley replied.

"What do you mean?" Stone asked.

"I was leaving for work and had put most of my things into my car and realized I forgot my lunch. I went back inside, and when I returned, my backpack and laptop were gone! I was only inside for two or three minutes at most, and in that length of time, some asshole stole my laptop. I called the police to report it and thought you were here to take my report."

Clayton and Stone glanced at each other, and then Stone said, "Please tell me you had it backed up somewhere."

"No. Anna gave it to me on an encrypted flash drive and asked me not to save it anywhere on the computer if someone tried to break into my computer remotely. Now, what's going on? Is Anna okay?"

Stone looked at Clayton, who gave her a slight nod and said, "It might be better if you have a seat."

"You're starting to scare me," Riley said, getting increasingly nervous.

"I'm afraid Anna's dead," Stone said.

"What?" Riley replied in shock, "How? What happened?"

"All I can tell you at this point in the investigation is she was murdered, and after she was murdered, someone broke into her apartment and stole all of her computer equipment," Clayton said matter of factly.

Riley half sat, and half fell back onto her couch in shock and sat there in silence for a moment. Then, with tears running down her face, Riley said, "You think it has something to do with the book. Don't you?"

"We do. And now that someone has come here and stolen your laptop also ... we're pretty sure of it." Clayton replied.

Stone sat on the couch beside Riley and asked, "Is there anything you can tell us about the book or what she might have been doing? Anything at all will help fill in the pieces."

Wiping tears off her face, Riley said, "Anna was obsessed with finding out the story of Jonathon Blackwood's murder. I was editing the book for her, so I can tell you a lot about what she found, but there is something she was keeping ... even from me."

Clayton sat in a chair and said, "Start from the beginning. Tell us everything, and don't leave anything out."

Riley took a deep breath and said, "Okay, as the story goes, Jonathon Blackwood and Peter Harrington were friends and grew up together even though the Harrington family didn't think too highly of the Blackwood family."

"Why was that?" Stone asked.

"The Harrington family was, and still is, very well off. Everybody knows they have money, and the old guard of the family lives on that twenty-acre estate on the lake."

"Okay, go on," Clayton replied.

Riley said, "Well, Anna became convinced that someone in the Harrington family, probably their oldest son, Theodore, killed Jonathon, especially after Peter was found dead."

"Why did Anna suspect Theodore?" Stone asked.

"Because Jonathon and Peter came up with a plan to buy a large tract of land on Lake Murray and put a resort on it, but they didn't have enough capital, so—"

Before she could finish, Clayton said, "They brought in Theodore, who, being the oldest, would have more money to invest."

Riley said, "Yeah, but that's when it all seemed to go south."

"What do you mean?" Stone asked.

"Since Theodore was the oldest, he was the typical spoiled little rich kid. Even though he came from money, Peter was the youngest and more hands-on working class. Peter and Jonathon got along better than he and his brother did. It seemed as if Theodore was always jealous of Peter for one reason or another."

Clayton said, "So, the three of them tried to buy this tract of land, and two of them ended up dead. Is that what I'm hearing?"

"Essentially, yes. We think Theodore killed Peter one night in a fight over the land deal. The police looked into Peter's death, and after a time, it appears that his family influenced the police not to look very hard because the whole thing quietly went away. Not long after, Theodore approached Jonathon about continuing the land sale with just the two of them. Theodore would put up more money and collect more of the payout."

"Well, what happened?"

"We don't know. The next thing we know, Jonathon is found dead floating in a boat on Lake Murray."

"And there's nothing else you can tell us about the book?" Stone asked.

"Well, there is one thing, but I'm not sure if it will help," Riley said.

"Anything will help," Stone replied.

"Anna wanted more information on the family, so she used her mother's maiden name and got a job working on the estate as a maid. One of the last times I spoke with Anna, she told me she found something shocking."

"What was it?"

"I don't know, she wouldn't say, but she did tell me she had proof of what she found."

"Did she say where or what the proof was?"

"Strangely enough, no. She only said that as long as someone remembered her birthday, it would be okay."

"What does that mean? Stone asked.

"I have no idea," Riley replied.

Stone and Clayton thanked Riley for talking to them, and as they stood up to leave, Clayton said, I think the next thing we need to do is have a little chat with Theodore Harrington."

"You're not going to be able to do that," Riley said, "He's dead too."

## 6

Clayton's mouth dropped, and he said, "What do you mean he's dead too?"

"After Jonathon Blackwood was murdered, police thought that it was suspicious that two out of the three people in this land deal were now dead, but, in my opinion, the police didn't look very hard. Anyway, Theodore laid low for a time, and then he started making business trips up and down the East Coast for the family. Theodore's plane went missing over the Atlantic on one of these trips and was never found."

Stone and Clayton looked at each other in shock, thanked Riley for her help again, and silently walked outside to their car. Before the car doors were closed, Stone said, "Apparently, Anna found something incriminating, and she was killed for it."

"My thoughts exactly," Clayton replied.

"Well, if that's the case, who in the hell killed Anna Blackwood?" Stone inquired.

"That is a mystery now, isn't it?" Clayton replied, "We need to go back to the office and talk with the Chief of Detectives. I want to fill him in on everything we've found. I have a sneaky suspicion that we may be heading down a dark road."

"Yeah, it might not be a bad idea to at least tell him what we've found," Stone replied.

Not long after returning to the Sheriff's Office, Clayton and Stone walked down the hallway and knocked on a door marked Chief of Detectives, Stephen Boone.

"Enter," the two detectives heard from the other side of the door.

Both detectives walked in, and Clayton asked, "Sir, can we have a word with you?"

Boone stopped working on his computer and smiled at seeing his oldest and newest detective working together, "Sure. What can I do for you two?"

Clayton and Stone took the next twenty minutes detailing what they had found in the case and where the case was leading them. After listening to the detectives, Boone took a deep breath and said, "Follow the facts no matter where they lead. Just know this ... even though they are not as powerful as they once were, the Harrington's still have some strong friends, so be careful, tread lightly, and let me know if you need anything."

About that time, Clayton's phone rang. He pulled the phone off his belt clip, looked at the caller, which read SLED, and said, "We may be getting ready to get some answers."

"Answer it," Boone said, clearly wanting to know the ballistics test results.

"This is Detective Clayton," he said as he pushed a button on his phone to turn on the speaker so Boone and Stone could also hear.

"This is Detective Wilson over at SLED, and I have some results for you on the ballistics for that bullet you brought me."

"My partner and I are anxiously awaiting your findings," Clayton replied.

"Although I can't say exactly what kind of gun fired the rounds, I can tell you that both bullets were, without a doubt, fired from the same gun. Also, both bullets are a unique eight-millimeter caliber."

"Eight-millimeter?" Boone asked, surprised.

"Strange ... I know," Wilson replied, "but I double-checked, and there is no doubt it's an eight-millimeter bullet."

"Why is that strange?" Stone asked.

Wilson replied, "Because there have only been a small number of pistols officially designated as eight-millimeter in caliber, and I believe the last one was the Japanese Nambu pistol that was last produced in 1944, I believe. The closest thing in the US is a .32, which won't work in the Nambu."

"So, we're talking about a very old weapon," Stone replied.

"Yeah, that and ammo, too," Wilson added.

"Okay, thank you," Clayton said.

"No problem, just do me a favor and let me know if you find out what type of weapon the rounds came from. I'm curious to know," Wilson replied.

"Sure, no problem," Clayton said before hanging up the phone.

"Now, what do we do?" Stone asked.

"We do what the boss said and follow the leads," Clayton replied, "but we're going to do it tomorrow."

"Good. Get out of my office then. I still have paperwork to do," Boone replied with a smile.

"Sure will," Clayton said with a chuckle.

After the two detectives went their separate ways for the night, Clayton stopped at his favorite sandwich shop to order a sandwich to take home. Clayton sat in the corner and checked an email on his phone while waiting.

In a few minutes, the person behind the counter brought his sandwich to the table and told him to have a good night. Clayton stood up, yawned, and walked out to his car. As he walked up to his car, he saw that the passenger-side back tire was flat. The tire was completely flat, and the entire valve stem had been cut off, making it necessary to replace it.

As he stood over his flat tire, the car in the next row, bumper to bumper with Clayton's car, cranked up, causing Clayton to look in that direction. As soon as Clayton looked up, the driver turned on his lights and hit his bright lights.

Now completely blinded, Clayton put an arm up to keep the car's bright lights out of his face, and as he did, Clayton noticed a dark four-door car quickly pulling out of the parking spot.

"Son of a bitch!" Clayton yelled, realizing too little too late that the car was the exact description of the car the witness had seen at Anna's apartment break-in.

As the car took off, Clayton could only watch and attempt to get a plate number. However, getting a plate number was impossible, considering he was still seeing spots from the car's high beams.

After the car was gone, Clayton spent thirty minutes changing the tire and thinking about what just happened. It could have been a coincidence, or ... it could have been a warning. Clayton decided he would rather be safe than sorry and called Stone to inform her of what had happened. After that, he went home for a quiet night.

STONE MET Clayton at the office the following morning with two fresh cups of hot coffee. Handing Clayton a cup, Stone asked, "What happened?"

Clayton took a sip and again recounted what happened with the flat tire. "And you're sure it wasn't an accident?" Stone asked.

"Nope, the valve stem was cut off cleanly. There was no way it was an accident," Clayton replied, "so from now on, we need to be extra vigilant."

"That we do," Stone replied, "so, what's on tap for today?"

"While changing my tire last night, I thought about something," Clayton said.

"What's that?" Stone asked.

Clayton replied, "Where did the boat Anna was found in come from? We know the boat was never re-registered after it was bought, and it was a small fishing boat. It wasn't a pleasure craft like you would assume the Harrington family would have. So, the question remains: where did the boat come from?"

"That's a good question. Let's see if we can find out." Stone said as she picked up the phone on her desk and dialed a number.

"Who are you calling?"

"I have a friend who works in the robbery unit. Maybe he's heard of something."

"A friend, huh?" Clayton asked with an evil little smirk.

"Yes, just a friend," Stone said as she started to talk to someone on the line.

Clayton smiled and prodded, "So, why are your cheeks turning red?"

Ignoring Clayton, Stone said, "Hi, David, this is Stone over in homicide. Can you tell me if any boats have been stolen on the lake in the past few days?"

Stone listened intently for a couple of minutes, then she grabbed a pen and began to write an address down on a sticky note.

She thanked whoever she was talking to, hung up and playfully smacked Clayton on the shoulder, and said, "Asshole."

Clayton chuckled and said, "Turnabout is fair play. Do you have something?"

"First of all, it's obvious that Coroner King likes you, and secondly, David and I were in the academy together, and he's married."

Still chuckling, Clayton asked, "Did you get something?"

"Actually, I did, and this could be good, too. As it turns out, a small boat was reported missing from a dock about the same time of the murder, and guess where the dock is."

"Where?"

"Several hundred yards just down the shore from the Harrington estate," Stone said, smiling.

"You have got to be kidding me!" Clayton replied, shocked.

"Nope. Not at all."

"In that case, let's talk to the property owner and then drop in at the Harrington's estate and see if we can rattle their cage a little."

"Are you sure that's wise?" Stone asked.

"Nope," Clayton shot back, "but it's all we have right now."

"What are we waiting for then? Let's go," Stone replied with an evil smile.

## 7

Thirty minutes after leaving the office, the detectives pulled up to a small house surrounded by a group of trees. The house was older and outdated compared to the rest of the surrounding homes.

As they pulled into the driveway, they noticed a weathered sign nailed to a tree at the end of the drive that stated NO TRESPASSING in large block letters.

"That's a rather ominous sign. Don't you think?" Stone asked.

"Yeah, but it's common up here on some of these back roads. People come up here trying to get a glimpse of the lake and have no problem with walking on other people's property to do it," Clayton said.

After parking, the pair got out and cautiously approached the front door of the house, ensuring to be on alert for anything out of the ordinary. Before they even reached the door, they saw an older man looking out of a nearby window, and as soon as they saw him in the window, he disappeared out of sight.

"That's not a good sign," Stone said, "somebody knows we're here."

"Yeah, I saw him too," Clayton replied, slowly pulling his coat away from his service weapon.

Just then, the door opened, and the same older man they saw in the window stood in the doorway of the house, smiled, and said, "Hi. Are you two from the sheriff's department?"

"Yes, sir. We are," Clayton replied, "Did you have a boat taken from your place?"

The old man said, "Sure did. I can't say exactly when, though. I only come up here about once a month or so to go fishing. The last time I saw it was when I was here about three weeks ago, and it was tied up at the pier."

"So, you weren't here a couple of nights ago?" Stone asked.

"Naw, I was in town. I just got up here last night and realized it was gone."

Clayton showed the man a picture he had taken on his phone of the boat's bow where the old registration numbers were and asked, "Is this your boat?"

"Looks like it," the man replied with a huff, "where did you find it?"

Clayton glanced at Stone and said, "It was found adrift in the lake. We're curious ... why have you not registered the boat since you bought it?"

"Didn't see the need. I only use it right around here, maybe one or two days out of the month, and when it gets cold, I don't even use it then."

"Can we see where the boat was tied up?" Stone asked.

"Sure, no problem. Follow me," the man said as he walked them around the back of his old home, saying, "My name is Tom, by the way."

"I'm Detective Clayton, and this is Detective Stone. It sure is beautiful up here."

"Yep, and it used to be peaceful, but not so much anymore since people have bought up all the land around here."

Tom walked the two detectives around back to a short yet well-built pier that went out into the lake for perhaps fifty or seventy-five feet.

As they walked to the end of the pier, Stone pointed down the bank and asked, "What's through those trees? It looks like it's open ground through there."

"That would be the back of the Harrington estate that backs up to the lake. Back when there was nothing out here, my folks bought up this tract of land, knowing the price would increase. I fell in love with it and just can't sell it."

"I understand why," Clayton said as he looked out over the lake, "It's simply beautiful here."

"Yep, it is. I have to ask. When can I get my boat back?"

"Right now, your boat is technically evidence in an open investigation. The sheriff's department will be holding it until the case is over, but when it's finished, we'll see that you get your boat returned to you ... providing you get it registered." Clayton replied.

"Deal," Tom said as they slowly walked back to the front of the older house.

As both detectives got into their car and backed out, Stone said, "That was easy enough. I'll bet Anna probably ran through those woods and onto Tom's pier from the Harrington estate. Don't you?"

"Yep, sure do. Now, let's go to the Harrington's estate and see if we can rattle somebody's cage," Clayton replied.

Clayton drove down the road a short distance and pulled up to an elaborate gate with a call box. Clayton rolled down the window and pressed the call button. Shortly after that, a voice was heard asking, "Can I help you?"

Clayton replied, "Yes, we're Lexington County sheriff's detectives, and we need to come in to talk to you about one of your employees."

Instead of a response, the gate simply swung open. Clayton pulled through the gate and followed the long driveway to a huge, well-manicured three-story home.

"Wow, this is night and day difference between this and the place we just left down the street," Stone said.

"Sure is," Clayton replied in awe.

As the pair approached the elaborate front door, it swung open, and a house staff member said, "Welcome to the Harrington Estate. Mrs. Harrington will see you in the sitting room. Right this way."

Clayton and Stone followed the person through the foyer and into a small yet well-furnished room for entertaining guests.

As they entered the room, an older lady sitting in a chair got up, walked over, and stuck her hand out to shake hands with the detectives. She used all the Southern charm she could muster, saying, "Good morning, I'm Beatrice Harrington, and welcome to the Harrington Estate. What can I do for you?"

Clayton and Stone introduced themselves, and Clayton said, "Ma'am, we're here about who we think is one of your employees, Miss Anna Watkins. Do you know her?"

Harrington said, "I wouldn't say I know her, but I am familiar with her. She has been working here for about a month, although I haven't seen her in a few days. Why? Has something happened?"

Momentarily ignoring the question, Stone pressed, "Ma'am, are there any other family members living here at this time?"

"Sadly, no. My husband, Reginald, passed away a few years ago, and all of my children have moved out. Why, what is this about?"

Stone glanced at Clayton and said, "Ma'am, I'm afraid Anna Watkins is dead."

Beatrice gasped and said in her deeply southern voice, "Oh, dear! What happened?"

"I'm afraid she was murdered," Clayton replied, monotoned.

"No, no, no! Not again!" Beatrice muttered, "It was hard enough to find someone to work out here after my son Theodore passed away. Now you're telling me there has been another death?"

"I'm sorry to say ... yes, it's true," Clayton said.

"Not only that, but we believe she was murdered very near here," Stone said coldly.

"What?" Beatrice said, appearing to be genuinely shocked.

Clayton pressed Beatrice and sternly asked, "Ma'am, do you own any guns, particularly old ones?"

"Guns?" Beatrice asked, shocked, "No, I don't know anything about guns. What is going on here?"

Ignoring the question momentarily, Stone asked, "What did you mean when you said not again?"

Beatrice replied, "About thirty years ago, Jonathon Blackwood and my youngest son Peter tried to do a land deal together for a large tract of land on the lake. I thought it was a bad idea and told them I wouldn't get involved from the start. They couldn't get the collateral, so my oldest son, Theodore, stepped in to help. That turned out to be a bad move for all concerned."

Even though he already knew most of the story, Clayton wanted to hear her version and asked, "What happened?"

"It all went to hell in a handbasket. That's what happened. The next thing I knew, Peter was dead. Police said somebody found him on the side of the road. He had either been hit by a car or beaten. It wasn't long after Peter died that Jonathon Blackwood was killed."

"You mean murdered. Don't you?" Stone corrected.

"Killed ... murdered ... it's all the same thing. Dead is dead," Beatrice said with a wave of the hand, "anyway, after that is when the rumors started."

"What rumors?" Stone asked.

"There was a terrible rumor that Theodore killed Peter in a fit of jealous rage, and Jonathon found out, so Theodore killed Jonathon, too. Then, there was a rumor that Jonathon killed Peter, and Theodore killed Jonathon out of revenge. Either way, it wasn't true and doesn't matter anymore since not too long after that, Theodore was killed in a plane crash. "What does that ancient history have to do with Anna Watkins?"

"Actually, it has everything to do with Anna's death because Anna used her mother's maiden name to get the job here with you. Her real name is ... Anna Blackwood."

Momentarily caught off guard, Stone and Clayton both saw the fleeting shocked expression on Beatrice's face then it was gone just as fast as it had appeared. "Why would she do that?" Beatrice asked.

Stone replied, "Ma'am, we're simply gathering information on a murder that very well could have happened on or near your property. Nothing more."

Beatrice called out, "Sam ... Sam, come in here a moment, would you please?"

At once, a middle-aged man dressed in a business suit walked to the door and said, "Yes, ma'am?"

"Be a dear and bring my purse in here. Would you?"

"Yes, ma'am," the man said before walking out, eyeing the two detectives.

Stone and Clayton simply looked at each other, and before either one could say anything, the man named Sam returned and handed Beatrice her purse. Stone and Clayton watched as Beatrice opened her purse, pulled out a business card, and said, "Here is my lawyer's information. If either of you have any more questions, please feel free to contact him at any time, day or night."

"Thank you, ma'am, for the information, but we're not finished speaking with you," Clayton replied sternly.

Beatrice's entire demeanor changed as she dropped the grand old southern charm, glared at the two detectives, and shot back, "But I am done speaking to you. You two showed up to my home and all but accused someone on my estate of murder. Now, I will be glad to forward the names of everyone who works here on the estate to your office, but that's all. Sam, please see to it that these two detectives leave the estate."

"Gladly," Sam said, motioning for the detectives to follow him back to the door.

As the man known as Sam turned to open the front door for the detectives, his jacket pulled away from his side long enough for Clayton to get a glance of a pocketknife clipped onto his side. "That's a nice-looking knife you've got," Clayton said, "I'll bet it's sharp, and what's that bulge under your jacket on the other side? You got a carry permit for it?"

The man, known as Sam, eyed Clayton and said, "It's sharp enough, and I don't need a carry permit on the estate. Have a good day."

Clayton smiled and said, "I'll bet it's even sharp enough to cut through a valve stem in one cut. Isn't it?"

Sam squared up to Clayton and asked sharply, "Just what do you mean by that?"

"You know exactly what I mean. Don't you?" Clayton said.

Sam softened his tone, smiled devilishly, and said, "I have no idea what you're talking about."

"Mind if I take a look at your weapon?" Clayton asked.

Sam eyed the two detectives warily and replied, "Not at all, careful though ... it's loaded."

Sam slowly reached in and pulled out his weapon, which turned out to be a beautifully made .45 caliber Colt. Clayton admired the pistol and said, "Colt 1911 Trophy Model, stainless steel finish with black and blue grips ... simply stunning."

"It shoots just as good as it looks, too," Sam replied smartly."

"I'm sure it does," Clayton said, glaring at Sam, "you have yourself a good day," Clayton said as he returned Sam's weapon to him.

"You too," Sam said as Clayton backed away from him.

After they returned to their car, Stone looked at Clayton and asked, "Do you think he was the guy who cut your valve stem?"

"I don't know," Clayton replied, "He's a pretty big boy. He doesn't strike me as the yes-man type. He could be the family's fixer. I just don't know."

"Then what was all that for at the door just now?" Stone asked.

"Just pushing buttons, that's all. Besides, I wanted to look at his gun," Clayton replied with an evil smile.

"It was a good thought, but there's no way that his gun killed Anna," Stone replied, "so ... now what do we do?"

Clayton replied, "Sam's gun was definitely not the gun that killed Anna. Let's go back to the office. Maybe by now, the DNA is back on the toothbrush we took from Anna's apartment. If so, we can call Anna's mom in and have a little chat without her parents around. Somehow, I get the feeling she would be more open to talking without her father being there."

"Sounds good to me," Stone said as her stomach let out a large gurgle.

"Hungry?" Clayton asked, smiling.

"Don't you know by now, I'm always hungry," Stone replied.

"It's between the breakfast and lunch crowd, so we should be able to get in fairly easy at Creekside if you want," Clayton offered.

"I was hoping you were gonna say that," Stone said with a smile. I want a cheeseburger and fries."

"That actually sounds good," Clayton replied, "their cheeseburgers are amazing! Next stop, Creekside Restaurant!"

## 8

Twenty minutes later, the pair walked into Creekside Restaurant to the waitress' ever cheerful, "Hey ya'll!"

"Hello," Stone said as she glanced at Clayton, who was smiling at his favorite waitress.

As the waitress walked with the detectives to a table near the front window, she asked, "What are you to getting today?"

"I think we're going to make it easy for you today, and both of us are going to have cheeseburgers with fries and no onions on either one," Clayton said with a smile.

"And you want your usual sweet teas to drink?" the waitress asked.

"Sure do," Stone said.

The waitress finished writing their order and said, "Okay, I'm going to put your order in, and I'll be back to check on ya in a few minutes."

"Thank you," Clayton said as he glanced at the waitress walking off to put the order in."

A few minutes later, both detectives saw Kirt, the owner, working hard in the kitchen. Kirt looked up for a moment and locked eyes with the detectives just long enough to give them a friendly wave and smile, then went right back to work.

After the waitress dropped off their drinks, Stone asked, "What do you think is happening?"

Clayton replied, "In short, I think Anna Blackwood used her mom's maiden name to get a job on the Harrington Estate for research on her book, and I believe she found something that ended up getting her killed. What that is, I have no idea, but one can only assume that it has something to do with the murder of Jonathon Blackwood."

Stone responded by saying, "Maybe she found out who actually committed the murder?"

Clayton shot back, "She found out something she shouldn't have, that's for sure. I have a sneaky suspicion that we will be arresting someone on the Harrington Estate before this is over."

"It sure seems that way," Stone replied.

After setting the plates down, the waitress asked, "Can I get anything else for ya?"

"We're good," Stone replied as they dug into their burgers.

In between bites, Stone said, "I have an idea."

"I'm listening," Clayton mumbled as he shoved several French fries into his mouth.

"We know for a fact that Anna was chased through the woods. Right?"

"Yeah, because her clothes were all picked and nicked like she had been running through the brush, and the bottoms of her pants and shoes were dirty," Clayton said.

"We can surmise Anna was chased from the Harrington Estate through the woods, where she found the neighbor's dock and ran out towards the boat," Stone said excitedly.

"I'm with ya so far," Clayton replied.

"So, we may be able to trace her path backward through the woods to the Harrington Estate. If we can do that, we can get a search warrant based on exigent circumstances."

"Can't do it," Clayton replied, "exigent circumstances require immediate attention, like preventing the destruction of evidence, like a drug dealer flushing his stash or something like that. Can't use exigent circumstances as a fishing expedition."

"Well, damn," Stone said dejectedly.

Clayton shot back, "Don't worry, we'll figure something out. We already know the same gun was used to fire both bullets, so if we can find the gun, we can get a search warrant that way. Eat up. We need to get back to the office."

"Why? We got something to do?" Stone asked.

"Yep, we're going to take a fresh look at everything from the beginning," Clayton said.

Once they finished eating and walked to the register to pay, Kirt walked to the pass-through window and asked, "Everything good?"

"Excellent as always!" Clayton replied with a smile.

"Good, glad to hear it!" Kirt replied with a smile and a wave.

AFTER LEAVING Creekside and returning to the office, both detectives spent the next hour laying out and reviewing everything they knew about the case.

Once they had everything laid out before them, Stone asked, "Don't you find it odd that all three individuals who were involved in the land deal thirty-three years ago died tragically while trying to make this land deal?"

"What are you thinking?" Clayton asked.

"I'm not sure. Maybe we're looking at this case wrong. Maybe it's about the land deal."

"What do you mean?"

"All the land at the lake has been gobbled up, but over thirty years ago, there was still land to be had. If someone had the wherewithal to buy a plot of land and hold on to it, today it would be worth ten times what they bought it for." Stone replied.

"If we could find out where the land was the three were going to buy and see what's on that property now; it may lead somewhere," Clayton said.

"Yeah, but that is a long shot at best," Stone replied.

Just then, the phone on Clayton's desk rang. Clayton answered the phone, listened momentarily, and said, "We'll be right out."

"What is it?" Stone asked.

"Hopefully, we just got lucky," Clayton said as he hopped up, "follow me."

"Where are we going?"

"To the lobby. Anna's mother just walked in with a small box and said she needed to talk to us."

Both quickly walked out to the front desk holding a brown box that was used to send documents through the mail. When Anabelle saw the detectives, she looked relieved and started rambling, "I just got this in the mail. Anna sent it before she died. I didn't know what to do with it, so I just brought it here."

"Have you opened it?" Clayton asked as Stone took the box from Anabelle.

"No, I haven't. I didn't know if I should, and to be quite frank with you, I was too scared to. I thought it might be important, so I brought it to you. I was hoping you would open it."

Stone took the box and said, "We'd be glad to open it for you. Besides, there could be evidence here that will help our case."

"Can I be there when you open it?" Anabelle asked.

"Sure, we'll open it now. Let's go into an office."

Stone and Clayton escorted Anabelle into an empty conference room, where Stone gingerly opened the box and cautiously dumped the contents onto the table. Something slid out of the box, wrapped in what appeared to be a cleaning rag.

Clayton put on gloves and gently unfolded the rag to find a cell phone and Anna's driver's license.

Anabelle recognized the phone as soon as she saw it, gasped, and said, "That's Anna's phone."

Clayton examined the phone and said, "It's turned off. She must have powered it off before putting it in the mail." Clayton held the button on the side of the phone, and before long, the password screen came on.

"Do you know the password?" Stone asked as he looked at Anabelle.

"No, sorry. I have no idea what it could be," Anabelle replied apologetically.

Clayton replied, "No problem. I got you covered on the password, but we need to obtain a search warrant for whatever is on the phone before we do anything."

"How could you know what the password is?" Stone asked.

"When we interviewed Riley, the friend, she told us that everything would be ok as long as somebody remembered Anna's birthday. I'd be willing to bet that Anna's birthday is the password that unlocks her phone," Clayton replied.

Over the next hour, Stone and Clayton did the required paperwork to get the search warrant for the phone that Anna had sent to her mom before she was murdered.

When the two were out of earshot of Anabelle, Stone said, "You know, by Anna sending that phone in the mail as she did, she knew she was in danger."

"Yep, and whatever is on that phone could very well be the break we need in the case," Clayton replied.

"Are you sure you want Anabelle to see what's on the phone?" Stone asked.

Clayton thought a moment and replied, "No, I don't, but I don't have the heart to tell her she can't see it either. After all, she did bring us the phone."

"I'll take care of it," Stone replied, "Let me talk to her for a moment alone."

"Not a problem," Clayton replied.

Stone walked back into the room where Anabelle was waiting and said, "We're having a little trouble finding a judge to sign off on a search warrant for a phone that simply showed up in the mail. "Why don't you go home where you'll be more comfortable, and we'll call you as soon as we have something?"

Anabelle thought momentarily and asked, "What ... what about Anna's phone? Will I get it back? Because I'd like to have it back."

"It may be some time, but everything will be returned to you," Stone said as she gently guided Anabelle toward the front lobby.

As Anabelle stopped at the lobby door, she asked, "Will ... will you at least tell me what was on the phone when you open it?"

"I will if I can, but I can't promise anything, especially if it concerns the case. I promise we will take great care of Anna's phone," Stone said compassionately.

Tears started welling up in Anabelle's eyes, and she said, "Thank you for being so nice to me."

Stone hugged her and said, "Don't worry. We're going to get to the bottom of this. Do you need me to have somebody take you home, or can you drive yourself?"

"I'll be fine," Annabelle muttered between wiping tears and crying spells.

As soon as Anabelle left, Stone quickly returned to where Clayton awaited her, "You ready to see what's in the phone?"

"Sure am," Stone replied excitedly.

Clayton typed Anna's birthday into the password field, and the phone opened on the first try. "We're in," Stone said, "check her photos and videos."

Clayton scrolled through the thousands of pictures until he reached the end of her picture roll. All the photos, except for the last dozen, were typical selfies with friends and family. However, the last ten or twelve photos were taken in a completely different setting.

Focusing on the last dozen photos, Stone and Clayton could tell that they were taken in a room with bare white walls, "Let me see something," Stone said as she took the phone from Clayton.

Clayton watched as Stone tapped a few buttons, then smiled, saying, "Good girl!"

"What is it?" Clayton asked.

Still smiling, Stone replied, "These last pictures are geotagged, meaning I know exactly where they were taken! That's why she sent us the phone!"

"Ok, where were they taken, as if I don't already know?" Clayton asked.

"You'd be right, too," Stone replied. "According to GPS, they were indeed taken on the Harrington Estate."

"Now all we have to do is figure out why these pictures were taken and why Anna thought they were important," Clayton said.

After going through all the photos one by one, a pattern began to appear. Each photo they were interested in had been taken at strange angles and positions as if they were taken discreetly or quickly. There was also a photograph of an older, unknown man taken from the side just as he walked out of a room.

"Now, why in the world do you suppose she took this picture?" Clayton asked, studying the picture of the man who appeared to be in his late fifties or early sixties.

"I have no idea, but she thought it was important," Stone replied.

On a hunch, Stone closed the photos app and opened the notes app. As soon as it opened, Stone found one word ... Erebus.

# 9

"What in the hell is Erebus?" Clayton asked.

"Let's find out," Stone said as she walked over to her computer and pulled up her favorite search engine, "Google always knows," she said with a smile.

With just a few taps, the name came right up, "And here it is," Stone said, "In Greek mythology, Erebus is the primordial god of darkness."

"Ok, I'm officially creeped out now," Clayton said.

"Yeah, me too," Stone said as she stared at the screen. After a moment, Stone looked at Clayton and asked, "What in the hell did this girl stumble on?"

"I have no idea, but whatever it was ... this could be what got her killed," Clayton replied.

For a moment or two, both sat there in utter silence, trying to put the new pieces of the puzzle together. Finally, Stone asked, "What if Anna was initially researching the Jonathon Blackwood murder and used her mother's maiden name to get a job on the estate and stumbled onto something else, and that's what got her killed, not the Blackwood murder?"

"Right now, I'd believe just about anything," Clayton replied.

"I have an idea," Stone said with an optimistic tone.

"What's that?" Clayton asked.

"Why don't we take the picture with the older man in it and run it through our facial recognition software to see if we get anything?"

"It's worth a shot," Clayton replied, "let's do it."

Stone uploaded the picture in question and let the program run; however, after an hour-long search, no results were found.

"Well, damn," Stone said dejectedly.

"Maybe we looked up the wrong thing," Clayton said, "try looking up that word you found in the notes ... Erebus."

"Might as well," Stone said as she typed the name into the search field, "what are you thinking?"

"I'm not sure, really. Anna made that note for a reason, so it was important to her," Clayton said, "and if she thought it was important ... we should too."

On a hunch, Clayton said, "Try putting that name in NCIC and see what happens."

Stone switched programs and again typed Erebus into the NCIC database ... then she paused before hitting enter.

"What's the hold-up?" Clayton asked.

"Nerves, I think. I'm unsure if I want to know what this search brings back."

"I understand, but we owe it to Anna to find out what happened to her and why."

Stone hit the enter key without another word and waited for the results to populate.

As soon as Stone hit the enter key, the results returned with zero hits.

"I knew it wasn't going to be that easy," Clayton replied.

"Pull up that photo of the older man on Anna's phone," Clayton said, "I want to take another look at him."

With a few taps, a photo appeared of the older man, and Stone asked, "What are you thinking?"

Thinking a moment before answering, Clayton said, "I'm not sure. Do we have any photos of Beatrice's husband? What was his name?"

"His name was Reginald, but he's dead. He died a few years ago, so that can't be him," Stone replied.

"No, but it could be one of his sons," Clayton reiterated.

"I suppose. There is a little family resemblance," Stone said, "The only son left is William, so it would have to be him."

"Let's run William Harrington down and see where he's at now just for shits and giggles."

"It may take a little time, but I can do it," Stone replied.

"Good. In the meantime, I will check into the land deal Jonathon attempted to put together thirty years ago," Clayton said.

"Why?" Stone asked, surprised.

"I can't help it. It's too much of a coincidence that all three people who were involved in that land deal died rather mysteriously," Clayton said.

Just then, the phone on Stone's desk rang. As soon as she picked it up, Stone looked over and made eye contact with Clayton, who could tell by the look on her face that something was going on.

Clayton listened to Stone say, "Yes, sir ... yes, sir. The name came up in a case we were working ... we will wait here for you." Without another word, she hung up the phone.

Clayton asked, "What was that about?"

"I think we got somebody's attention with that NCIC search. That was Special Agent Peter Davenport with the FBI."

"FBI?" Clayton asked, shocked.

"Yep, and he wanted to know why I just did that NCIC search for Erebus."

"What did he say?"

"In short, he said he was on his way to talk to us in person about Erebus. What in the hell is going on?"

"I don't know, but we need to loop in the boss before the FBI arrives, that's for sure." Clayton said, "Let's go."

Both walked over and knocked on the boss's door, and after hearing, "Enter," they opened the door and walked in, making sure to close the door behind them.

"This can't be good," Boone said as he read their faces, "what can I do for you both?"

Clayton said, "We have a problem."

"Oh, and what's that?" Boone asked.

"It's an FBI problem," Clayton said.

"What are you talking about? Does this have something to do with the case you two have been working on?"

"Yeah, and we ran across the name Erebus, and when we ran it through NCIC, five minutes later, the FBI called asking why we were researching that name. Stone told them the name came up in an investigation, and now they're sending an agent over to talk with us."

"If the FBI is sending an agent to talk to you, that means you have stumbled on an open investigation or something like that," Boone replied.

"Precisely why we came to tell you," Clayton said, "we have no idea what we've gotten ourselves into and wanted you to be aware."

"It's good that you did. Give me a call when this agent shows up. I want to be there."

"Will do, boss," Clayton said as he and Stone left Boone's office.

TWENTY MINUTES LATER, Stone got a call from the lobby that an FBI agent was there to see her. Stone looked over at Clayton and said, "He's here. Let's go."

Stone and Clayton hopped up from their desks and walked out to the lobby, where they saw a middle-aged man in a grey business suit waiting for them.

As soon as they walked out, the man glanced at them and asked, "Detective Stone?"

Smiling, Stone said, "Yes, that's me, and this is my partner Detective Clayton. Are you from the FBI?"

The man smiled as he shook hands with Stone and Clayton, then pulled his credentials out to verify who he was.

After showing his credentials, he said, "I'm Special Agent Peter Davenport. Do you have somewhere we could talk in private?"

"Yes, of course, follow me," Stone said with a sly smile.

Davenport followed Stone into a conference room while Clayton went to get Chief of Detectives Boone. Clayton returned a few moments later with Boone, who introduced himself to Davenport and said, "So, what's this all about?"

"In a word ... Erebus," Davenport replied with a New Yorker's accent.

"We figured as much, but what or who exactly is Erebus?" Stone asked.

"That's the thing ... we don't know," Davenport replied casually as he leaned back in his chair. "Why are you looking into the name?"

"That's not how this works," Boone replied sternly, "Now, you tell me what my detectives have come across, and they will share with you what they know."

Davenport momentarily thought about what Boone said, then replied, "Okay, we have a deal. In the fifties, a prolific and exceptional art thief worked his way across the United States and Europe. As far as we can tell, his career started out west in California, and over the years, he moved East. There were a few heists in Europe also attributed to Erebus as well."

"Okay, we're with you so far," Boone replied.

"Well, his last known job was in 1960 in Atlanta, Georgia, where he and at least two accomplices broke into a museum and stole over a dozen paintings by multiple famous artists. Later that day, a burnt-out van was recovered outside of Atlanta with two victims inside. We suspect the van was the getaway vehicle, and the two victims were the accomplices, but we were never able to prove anything."

"You still haven't told us what that has to do with our case," Clayton replied.

"I'm getting to it," Davenport said, "you needed the backstory before it all made sense. We know for a fact that the art thief managed at least twelve break-ins because he left a calling card on

the way out. He left a literal business card with one word on it ...
Erebus."

"Now it's starting to make sense," Stone replied, "you guys must
have had it flagged, so as soon as I initiated the search, you knew
about it."

"Exactly, and considering how close we are to his last known
heist, my bosses sent me." Davenport replied, "So, your turn. Why are
you looking into Erebus?"

Stone replied, "As I told you on the phone, we are looking into a
murder, and the name came up along the way."

"It did?" Davenport asked.

Clayton tapped Stone under the table and said, "Yes, we're not
sure what the meaning is yet. We recovered the murder victim's cell-
phone, and the name Erebus was typed into the phone as a note.
We're not sure what, if any, bearing it has on the case."

Davenport replied, "I see. Was there anything else of interest on
the phone?"

Before Stone could say anything, Clayton jumped in and said,
"Actually, there was. We have a photograph of a man. He's not old
enough to be your art thief, but we don't know who he is either."

"I can help with that," Davenport said, "If you send me the
picture, I'll run it through our facial recognition software, which is
much better than what you have."

"I was hoping you were going to say that," Clayton said as he
glanced at Boone and Stone.

"What was that look for?" Davenport asked.

"Oh, nothing," Clayton replied, smiling, "just happy to have your
help on this case because this has been a strange case from the start,
that's for sure."

Davenport looked at Clayton cautiously and asked, "And you're
sure there was nothing else on the phone?"

"No ... nothing that is of any use," Clayton said with a straight
face, "just a bunch of random shots."

"Ok, well, if you send me the picture, I'll be glad to check into it
for you," Davenport said as he stood up to leave.

Stone's cheeks flushed as she said, "Leave me a card with your contact information on it, and I will send it right on over."

Davenport stared at Clayton and said, "And let me know if you find anything useful."

"You will be our first call," Clayton replied.

After Davenport gave Stone his card, he stepped into the hallway and said, "I'll give you a call when I know something."

"Thanks again," Stone said as Davenport walked off towards the lobby.

Once they were sure Davenport was gone, Stone smiled at Clayton and said, "He's handsome. Ok, so, why did we lie to the FBI?"

Clayton smiled deviously and said, "Technically, I didn't. There were just a bunch of random shots. Put it like this: Special Agent Davenport just gave us a clue, and besides, if we had told him about the paintings in those last pictures, he would have swooped in and taken over the case."

"Why would they have done that?" Stone asked.

Clayton looked at Boone and said, "Rookies ... put it like this, if what Davenport said is accurate, and we have no reason not to believe it, it's at least possible that somebody in that family either was Erebus or was dealing in art that Erebus could have stolen."

"That was good thinking," Boone said with a smile, "the last thing we need is an FBI task force here looking into an art ring while you two are trying to solve this murder."

"Precisely," Clayton replied, "we may have been looking at this case completely wrong. Stone, make sure you send that picture to Special Agent Davenport, but *only* the picture of the unknown man."

"I'll do it right now. After that, then what do we do?"

Clayton thought momentarily and asked, "Boss, can you quietly get us some information on the museum robbery Davenport was talking about?"

"Sure, no problem. It could take a little time, though. I have a friend who works in Atlanta. Anything else?"

Clayton thought momentarily, then asked, "Actually, there is. Do you know anyone we can trust who knows about paintings?"

"No, I don't, but I'm sure somebody at USC can help you. What are you thinking?"

"What I'm thinking is, Anna Blackwood started researching the murder of Jonathon Blackwood thirty-three years ago, and she uncovered much more than she bargained for, and that's what got her killed."

Stone smiled and said, "Either Anna realized the artwork was stolen, or she found out who Erebus was, but that still leaves our mystery man in the picture. What does he have to do with anything?"

"There's only one way to find out. Send that picture to Special Agent Davenport, and let's see. In the meantime, I want to find someone who knows art and can tell us about the art in Anna's phone."

"Can't we do a reverse image search?" Stone asked.

Clayton replied with a wink, "We could, but I'd bet if we do that the next time we see Special Agent Davenport, he wouldn't be so friendly."

## 10

Stone and Clayton entered the University of South Carolina art department one hour after printing the art pictures on Anna's phone. Chief Boone had called ahead and arranged a meeting with the head of the department, Dr. William Peterson.

Once the detectives finally found his office, they found that the door was open and an older gentleman with grey hair, and round wire-rimmed glasses seated behind a messy desk.

"Are you Dr. William Peterson?" Clayton asked.

Looking up from the papers he was grading, the older man smiled and said, "Ah, yes. You two must be the detectives I received the phone call about. Come on in. How can I help you?"

Once they shook hands, Dr. Peterson motioned for them to have a seat and asked, "What can I do for you two today?"

Clayton said, "We are looking into a case that possibly involves art. We want to show you some photographs and see if you recognize any of the art, but before we do that, I must tell you that this is an ongoing case, and you are not to talk to anyone else about what we discuss."

"That will not be a problem," Peterson said.

Clayton handed Dr. Peterson a form and said, "I must insist that you sign this confidentiality agreement stating that you will not talk about what we discuss because of the sensitive nature of this investigation. I have to make it absolutely clear ... if you discuss anything we talk about, we will come back, and we will charge you with impeding our investigation. Is that understood?"

"Detective Clayton, I understand and would gladly lend my expertise with whatever you require," Dr. Peterson replied.

Stone handed Peterson the photos, and as he went through the pictures one by one, his eyes widened with surprise and shock. After repeatedly reviewing the pictures, Peterson asked, "How... where did you get these?"

Stone replied, "They are part of an investigation. What can you tell us about them?"

Admiring the pieces again, Peterson said, "I can tell you these appear to be artwork painted by masters of their time. I see a Renoir and van Gogh, at the very least. Neither of which I recognize. With that being said, of course, I can't tell if they're original or not, but if they are, they could be worth millions."

"For all of them?" Stone asked.

"No ... each," Peterson replied, smiling, "and if one happens to be an unknown or a quote-unquote lost work, it could be in the hundreds of millions."

"How would it affect the value of the paintings if they were stolen?" Stone asked.

"It depends. There is a black market for art, but you have to know who to go to and realize that the prices would be reduced. However, if you get the right bidders in the right place, at the right time, and they are bidding against each other, a piece of art could go very high, especially these days."

Dr. Peterson got up, walked over to a shelf full of books, and slowly started thumbing through several books, looking back and forth between the printouts and the pictures in his books while Clayton and Stone looked on.

After nearly thirty minutes, Dr. Peterson said, "Some of these paintings I can find no reference to at all, while others make reference to being either lost or stolen over time. If these are real master-pieces, you have an amazing find that will stun the art world."

"Great. Thank you, Dr. Peterson," Clayton said monotoned.

Clayton and Stone thanked Dr. Peterson for his help and again reminded him not to speak to anyone about what they had discussed. As they returned to their car, Clayton said, "I think we have been looking at this case entirely wrong."

"What do you mean?" Stone asked.

Clayton said, "Look at the pictures that Anna took on her phone. Except for the one picture with the unidentified man, the photos are all artworks."

Stone asked, "Maybe she liked the art?"

Clayton thought momentarily and said, "Could be ... but I don't think so. Look at how the pictures are taken. Some are very crooked, and some are not even remotely centered. The way the pictures are snapped, it's not like you're in a museum and have lots of time to get the perfect shot. These pictures were snapped in a hurry as if Anna didn't have a lot of time to snap the pictures."

"So, what are you thinking?" Stone asked.

Clayton paused and said, "I think we need to get back to the office and talk to Boone. That's what I think."

After stopping for a bite to eat, the two detectives returned to the office and checked in with Boone. Once they filled Boone in on what Dr. Peterson had told them, Boone said, "Well, I have something for the both of you also."

"Was your contact in Atlanta able to help us out?" Stone asked.

"Yes, but it's not much use. The file basically said what Special Agent Davenport told us when he was here. There were at least three individuals, maybe more, and they came in through a skylight that was being repaired. Apparently, they broke into the abandoned building next door, got to the roof, and roped across the alleyway to the museum roof."

Clayton surmised, "From there, it must have been a straight shot through the skylight to the floor below."

All three were silent for a moment, and then Boone said what they were all thinking, "I hate to say it, but we need to call Special Agent Davenport back. I think we're going to need his help."

"I was afraid you were gonna say that," Clayton said with a huff, "you know he's going to be pissed about the phone. Right?"

"Yeah ... probably, but I'm sure you'll think of something," Boone said with an evil grin.

"Gee, thanks," Clayton said, rolling his eyes at Boone.

"Since I talked to him first, I'll call him," Stone said.

Clayton grinned at Boone and said, "Works for me because you seem to have built a ... rapport with Special Agent Davenport."

Stone's eyes widened as she blushed again, but this time, it was because Clayton all but told Boone that she liked Davenport. "Hey!" Stone said as she playfully smacked Clayton on the shoulder, "I just said he's handsome ... unlike the flirting you and Courtney King were doing."

Boone's eyes widened, and he grinned from ear to ear at the friendly banter between the two and said, "Whoa there! Shots fired! I'm not sure I need or want to hear any more of this! Now get out of my office. I have work to do. Just keep me in the loop and let me know if you need anything."

"Will do," Clayton replied.

Stone went back to her desk to call Special Agent Davenport. He picked up on the second ring and said, "I was just about to call you."

"You were? Why's that?" Stone asked.

"I got a hit on your mystery man in the photo," Davenport said.

"Do tell," Stone replied excitedly.

"Not sure if it'll help, but his name is Dominick Winters. Strangely, he owns an investment firm in Miami, Florida."

"I see what you mean. I have no idea how that might fit. Maybe he's catering to a client or something," Stone said.

"Not sure. You weren't calling just for that, were you?" Davenport asked with a hint of optimism in his voice.

"Actually, I wasn't. I was hoping you could swing by here sometime. Clayton and I need to discuss something with you."

"Oh, I see," Davenport replied with a tinge of jealousy at hearing Clayton's name, "mind if I ask what about?"

Picking up on Davenport's change in tone, Stone said, "The case, of course ... among other things."

"I'm booked solid for the rest of the day but can make it over at about ten tomorrow morning," Davenport replied.

Stone said, "Can't wait." In a moment of panic, she realized what she had said and added, "To talk about the case, I mean."

Davenport chuckled and said slyly, "Yeah, sure ... I knew what you meant."

As Stone hung up the phone, Clayton walked over and asked, "Why are your cheeks so red?"

"Oh, I just embarrassed the shit out of myself with Agent Davenport, that's all," Stone said, flustered.

"How? Or do I want to know?"

"Nope, you don't want to know," Stone said as she buried her face in her hands.

It took the better part of the afternoon doing monotonous work, but eventually, Stone and Clayton determined that William Harrington, Beatrice's only surviving son, has been living in California for the past few decades, where he recently retired as a banker of all things and rarely returns to South Carolina.

"Well, another suspect crossed off the list," Stone said.

"Yes, but we could still benefit from a chat with William," Clayton shot back.

"How do you figure?" Stone asked quizzically.

Clayton said, "Look at it like this: humans are social creatures and mostly stay near family. Now, William is as far away as he can get from the rest of his family and still be on the same continent. One has to wonder why, now don't we?"

Stone thought momentarily, and then a smile crept across her face, "He must know something."

"Yes, indeed," Clayton said, "maybe not about the murder, but he can give insight into the family."

"Do we have contact information for Mr. Harrington?" Stone asked.

"We sure do. We next need to see if he would be willing to talk with us."

"And just how are we going to do that?" Stone asked.

"We gotta get Boone involved, but hopefully, we can get the local police in California involved to make contact and see if he would be willing to talk."

"Sounds like a plan. Let's try it." Stone replied.

Both detectives went over to Boone's office and walked in. Boone looked up from his computer and asked, "What can I do for you two?"

Clayton said, "Remember when you said if we need anything, to let you know."

"Yeah," Boone replied warily.

"Well, we need some help," Clayton responded.

"With what?"

"We need help contacting someone in the Harrington family," Clayton said.

"Why do you need my help for that?" Boone asked, sensing that the other shoe was about to drop.

"Well, here's the thing, boss ... he's in California."

"And just how in the hell is this Harrington going to be of assistance to your case?"

About that time, Stone jumped into the conversation and said, "That's the thing, we're not really sure. We know from his records that he moved to California after Jonathon Blackwood was murdered. We don't know why. If we can get an interview with him, we can either cross him off the list or—"

"Consider him a suspect," Boone said, finishing Stone's statement.

Boone leaned back in his chair and said, "Okay, let me make a few calls and see what I can do. Considering the time difference between

California and here, I doubt it will be today, though. Leave the contact information with me, and I'll get back to you."

"That's not a problem," Clayton replied, satisfied with Boone's answer.

Twenty minutes later, Boone found both detectives at their desks and said, "Okay, I got in touch with the local police department where he lives, and they're sending a car now to see if he would be willing to come in for a talk. I've already faxed the appropriate paperwork for him to sign if he should be willing to come in and talk."

"That's perfect! Thanks, boss!" Clayton said excitedly.

"Don't thank me yet. Let's see what happens. They will let me know what's happening in about half an hour, so don't leave. I know it's getting late, but it's three hours earlier there."

Clayton said, "Not a problem. Does anybody want a pizza while we wait? I'm buying."

Boone smiled and said, "You had me at pizza."

## 11

Crescent City, California

Officer Marcus Hernandez pulled up to a small, well-kept home in a quiet part of the town and hopped out of his patrol vehicle. He radioed that he was at the address in question and made a mental note that the person's car he was trying to contact was in the driveway.

Even though Hernandez was simply contacting the person inside, he always felt uneasy when it came to walking up to someone's front door, especially when he couldn't see inside, as was the case this time.

Hernandez stepped onto the front porch, rang the doorbell, and stepped back off the porch to separate himself from whoever opened the door.

He wouldn't have long to wait as he heard footsteps approaching the door. A middle-aged man with salt and pepper-colored hair opened the door and asked, "Yes? How can I help you, officer?"

Officer Hernandez smiled and said, "Hi, please excuse the intrusion, but are you, William Harrington?"

"Yes, that's me," Harrington replied, confused. "What's this about?"

"Mr. Harrington, I was asked to contact you about your family in

South Carolina. I was asked if you would be willing to return to the station with me and talk to some detectives in South Carolina."

"I haven't been to South Carolina in years. I don't know what information I could possibly offer. Do you know what it's concerning?"

Hernandez replied, "No, sir. I'm sorry, I don't know. All I was asked to do was come see if you would be willing to chat with some detectives."

"When?" Harrington asked.

"Actually ... they would like to speak with you now if it is at all possible," Hernandez replied.

"Very well, let me get my sweater," Harrington replied.

"Before we go, sir, If it's not too much trouble, I'd like to have a look at your identification. I need to verify that you are the William Harrington I was sent to talk to."

"Very well," Harrington said as he pulled out his wallet and showed Officer Hernandez his identification.

"Very well, sir. Right this way," Hernandez said as he escorted Harrington to his police car, making sure to put Harrington in the front seat with him.

After a quick ten-minute ride through the quaint town, Hernandez pulled up to their police department, escorted William Harrington into a conference room, and introduced him to a Crescent City Detective named Samuel Grant.

Detective Grant, a middle-aged man with a military-style flat top buzz cut, stood up and stuck out his massive hand to shake with Harrington and said, "Thank you for coming out to talk with us on such short notice."

Harrington returned the handshake and said, "It's no trouble at all, but I don't know what good it will do since I rarely go back to South Carolina and have very little to do with the rest of the family."

Grant offered Harrington a cup of coffee, which he politely declined. Then Grant said, "Before we begin, I need you to sign a paper for me. I know Officer Hernandez verified your identity, but this is a statement to that effect, saying that you are who you say you are."

"Very well," Harrington said as he looked over the paper and signed it.

After signing the paper and pushing it across the table to Detective Grant, he began, "Ok, so by now, I'm sure you're wondering why you've been brought here."

"The thought has crossed my mind," Harrington said with a smile.

Grant said, "We have a conference call set up with a couple of detectives from South Carolina, and they would like to speak with you about a case. If you give me a moment, I will dial in, and you will be able to see them on the screen at the end of the table."

It took Grant only one try to dial into the video conference. As soon as he did, an image appeared on the big screen at the end of the conference room table.

When the image appeared, Grant and Harrington could see an older man and a younger woman on the screen. Both waved and introduced themselves as Detectives Clayton and Stone. Grant then introduced himself and Mr. Harrington.

After the formalities, Clayton said, "First of all, Mr. Harrington, thank you for taking the time to meet with us, and thank you, Detective Grant, for helping to arrange all of this."

Mr. Harrington interrupted Clayton, saying, "First, tell me what's happening. I haven't been back to South Carolina in years, and I have no idea what's going on."

Clayton replied, "Earlier in the week, the body of a young woman was found floating in a boat on Lake Murray. As it turns out, the young woman's name was Anna Blackwood. Our investigation revealed that she was working on your family's estate."

"That can't be correct," Harrington stated, "the family would never hire a Blackwood."

"Why's that?" Stone asked, jumping into the conversation.

"Because the Harrington and Blackwood families have been at odds for the past thirty years, if not longer," Harrington said.

Clayton replied, "Our investigation revealed that she was working there under her mother's maiden name, and that is how she got the job. We feel she found something or saw something she shouldn't have."

Harrington chuckled and said, "And you think I might know what that is? Detective Clayton, I moved out here in the nineties and have done my best to avoid all that family drama."

Sensing an opening, Clayton leaned forward and replied, "We figured as much ... and that is precisely why we wanted to talk to you."

"I don't follow. What do you mean?" Harrington asked.

Stone said, "Mr. Harrington, Anna was doing research for a tell-all book about Jonathon Blackwood's murder thirty-three years ago, and we believe she found out something she shouldn't have."

Harrington was silent momentarily, looked down at the table, and quietly said, "I see."

Stone asked, "Mr. Harrington, your whole demeanor just changed. What is it?"

Harrington took a deep breath and said, "I haven't heard that name in a long time. I had hoped I had put all that behind me. That's all."

"All of what?" Stone asked sympathetically.

After a moment of silence, Harrington said, "It's hard to talk about, considering the fact that it's my own blood, but that family is rotten to the core."

About that time, Detective Grant, sitting beside Harrington, said, "Mr. Harrington, we can see you are bothered by something. Tell us what you know. I assure you that you will feel better to talk about it and get it out in the open."

Harrington took a deep breath and said, "Detective Clayton, my family has an affinity for two things, none of which I share."

"And what are they," Clayton asked.

Harrington said, "Buying real estate and fine art."

Upon hearing this, Clayton and Stone's eyes lit up, and they glanced at each other, trying to keep a straight face. "What do you mean fine art?" Clayton asked.

"Oh, yes," Harrington replied, "my father was always going off on a business trip buying real estate and coming home with a new piece of artwork. He would buy and sell art pieces and real estate to pay for the artwork. He was quite good at it."

"I see," Clayton said as he wrote everything down even though it was all being recorded. "Now, Mr. Harrington, I'm going to be very blunt and ask you a question."

"I've got nothing to hide. Ask away," Harrington replied.

Clayton stared at the screen and asked, "Do you know who killed Jonathon Blackwood or what happened to your brother Peter?"

Harrington's face went white as a ghost at the mention of Peter's name, and he said, "There's another name I haven't heard in a very long time."

After another moment of awkward silence, Harrington replied, "I truly don't know what happened to Peter or Jonathon Blackwood ... but I have my suspicions."

"Which are what?" Stone pressed.

Harrington looked off into space for a moment as if he were reliving an old memory, then said, "I don't suppose it matters anymore now that he's gone."

"Who's gone?" Stone asked.

"My brother Theodore. He was the oldest child but had no interest in real estate. His passion was investing, and he was good at it. While father was alive, he took Peter, the youngest, under his wing and taught him about real estate. Because of this, Theodore was always jealous of Peter."

"So, Theodore felt jaded because your father took an interest in the youngest son, Peter?" Clayton asked.

"That's correct. Anyway, over the course of several months, Peter and Jonathon Blackwood, who were friends, got together and attempted to buy a large plot of land on Lake Murray, but they didn't have the capital. They tried my father first, but he insisted they figure it out on their own. So, they went to my oldest brother Theodore, whom they knew had the money."

Clayton started to understand what Harrington was getting at and asked what everyone was thinking, "Did something happen between Theodore and Peter? Did Theodore kill Peter?"

With tears streaming down his face, William Harrington said, "I didn't think so ... at first. There were all sorts of rumors swirling around the family, but when Jonathon ended up getting murdered a few months later, I knew."

"You knew what?" Stone pressed.

Now barely able to look at the screen, Harrington said, "You must keep in mind that back then, my family knew many people and was once quite powerful." Harrington took another deep breath and continued, "Peter died on a deserted road on the land they wanted to buy. I believe Peter took Theodore out there to show him the property. They had a fight about something, and Theodore killed him."

"Then Theodore came home and told your parents, who, although grieving, paid off some people to ensure it looked like an accident," Clayton surmised.

"That is my assumption. I remember a lot of hushed conversations and such that I was not privy to at the time. After Peter's funeral, everyone stopped talking about it, and before long ... it just went away."

Clayton pressed Harrington, saying, "Theodore must have either tried to keep the business deal going or take over the business deal altogether, which somehow led to Jonathon Blackwood's murder."

Harrington said, "Again, it's just my suspicion, but many people knew about the supposed land deal, and now, with two out of the three dead, there was no way to keep it quiet. Theodore stayed on the estate for a while and started handling the family's business deals out of state. It was on one of these trips to Florida, I believe, that his plane disappeared."

Stone perked up at hearing that Theodore's plane disappeared on a trip to Florida and asked, "Are you sure Theodore's plane disappeared on a trip to Florida?"

"Quite sure. Why?" Harrington asked.

Ignoring Harrington's question, Stone played a hunch and asked, "Do you ever recall seeing a gun on the estate?"

Harrington thought momentarily and said, "Yes, Father brought one back from Japan at the war's end. I do not know if it's still around or if it even fires. I haven't seen it since I was young, but I remember one being there."

Clayton started to say something else, but Stone tapped him on the arm and said, "I think we have enough. Mr. Harrington, thank you for talking with us. We may need to ask another question or two at a later date, though."

"That would be fine," Harrington said.

Stone and Clayton thanked Detective Grant for setting up the interview and said they would be in touch if they needed anything else.

As soon as the conference call ended, Clayton looked at Stone and asked, "Ok, so what gives?"

"We need to do some research to make sure everything lines up like I suspect it will. I want to be sure when Special Agent Davenport arrives in the morning."

"What kind of research?"

Stone opened the file folder and shuffled through some papers until she found the photograph of the older man from Anna's phone. Stone held up the photo, smiled, and said, "This kind of research."

Clayton said, "I know I'm getting old, but you're not making any sense whatsoever right now."

Stone smiled and said, "Everything just fell into place. We need to fill in Boone on everything because he needs to be in the meeting with Special Agent Davenport in the morning."

## 12

T he following morning, Special Agent Davenport showed up right on time. However, Chief of Detectives Boone was tied up in a meeting and would not be available for at least an hour. Stone suggested that the three get breakfast when they told Davenport that Boone wanted to sit in on the meeting.

"Sounds good to me," Davenport said, "I haven't eaten yet. Where did you have in mind?"

Clayton looked at Stone and said, "The usual?"

"My thoughts exactly," Stone replied with a smile.

Not long afterward, the three pulled into the parking lot of the Old Mill and walked up the sidewalk to Creekside Restaurant, where they were greeted with the usual friendly, "Hey ya'll!" from the hostess.

Once they were shown to their table, all three ordered coffee and looked over the menu, making small talk while waiting for Clayton's favorite waitress to return.

Stone ordered her usual ham and cheese omelet with hash browns, while Clayton and Davenport ordered the breakfast bowls with hash browns, eggs, and bacon.

After the waitress left, Davenport said, "Ok, guys, what's going on?" I know a suck-up when I see one."

Clayton and Stone looked at each other, and Stone said, "Hey, you're the senior detective. You tell him."

"Tell me what?" Davenport asked warily.

Clayton said, "Look, I've had run-ins before with the feds, and I needed to be sure you weren't going to come in and try to poach my case."

"This already sounds bad," Davenport replied.

Clayton said, "I wasn't completely honest with you about the phone. There were several more photos on the phone that I chose not to tell you about. We didn't know what they meant at first until we talked to you, and now ... it all makes sense, but we need your help to prove it."

"What in the hell do you mean you didn't tell me everything? Don't you know I was acting in good faith, and I could have come in here with a warrant and taken the phone."

"As I said, we didn't know what the photos were about—but now I think your case and ours are connected."

The waitress returned with their food about that time, and Stone mumbled, "Thank God for small favors."

Davenport heard Stone and said, "Don't thank him yet. This isn't over."

The three dug into their meals, and after they finished eating, Davenport said, "Thanks for breakfast. Since you're sucking up, I assume you're paying."

Clayton chuckled and said, "Of course."

After paying, the three walked silently to Clayton's car, and as soon as the doors were closed, Davenport asked, "So, what were the other photos?"

Clayton paused momentarily and said, "Along with the photo of the older gentleman we showed you, there were about ten or eleven more photos of what we thought were random shots, but later we realized that they all had one thing in common."

"Which was what?" Davenport asked.

"Artwork," Clayton replied.

"What in the hell do you mean artwork?" Davenport nearly shouted.

Clayton said, "The photos were taken in such a way that we didn't realize it at first. We dismissed them as random or test shots, perhaps."

Davenport shook his head in disbelief and mumbled to himself, "Son of a bitch."

TWENTY MINUTES LATER, after arriving back at their office, Chief of Detectives Boone walked into the conference room where Clayton, Stone, and Davenport were. As soon as he walked in, Boone noticed the scowl on Davenport's face, and Boone said, "I assume he knows about the pictures."

"Yep," Stone said.

"And I'm not happy about it either," Davenport said smugly, "but if what Clayton says is true ... all will be forgiven. Now, what's going on?"

Stone handed Davenport printouts of the photos on Anna's phone and said, "Here are the rest of the pictures."

"Davenport's eyes widened as he looked through the pictures one by one. "This is definitely how our two cases are connected."

"How do you know?" Stone asked.

Handing the pictures back to Stone, Davenport grinned evilly and said, "To be honest, I held a little back also."

"I should have known," Clayton said with a huff, "what did you hold back?"

Davenport replied, "I can say that the FBI has been cracking down on art theft since the economy has been so volatile in the past few years."

Before he could say anything else, Stone asked, "What are you talking about?"

Davenport replied, "What I mean is the economy goes up and

down with the wind. Everybody knows that, but artwork, especially rare artwork, is bought and sold on the black market like a commodity. The only difference is it's more stable. If anything, the prices steadily go up."

Clayton said, "But someone we talked to told us that stolen paintings were nearly worthless since they couldn't legally be sold."

"Legally is the operative word," Davenport said. "Let's just say that this is not the first time the Harrington name has come up concerning artwork."

Boone, who had been silent until now, sat up and said, "Oh, really now?"

"Yes. All I can say is at one time, we had Reginald Harrington on film standing in the background of a black-market art deal in California."

"So, why didn't you do anything?" Stone asked.

"He was just in the background. He didn't try to buy or sell anything. He was merely watching along with several other individuals whom we either have not disclosed or can't identify."

"What about now?" Boone asked. "With the pictures on that phone that were geotagged from the estate, can that get you a warrant to have a look around the property?"

"Maybe, but we need a sure-fire thing to get our foot in the door," Davenport replied, "and as soon as the judge hears the phone was sent in the mail by a dead girl ... I'm not sure he'd go for it."

Stone glanced at Clayton and asked, "What if we have a way in? We'll need your help, but it could pay off for both of our investigations."

Davenport replied, "I'm listening."

Clayton looked at Stone and said, "Tell him, you're the one who came up with it."

"Tell me what?" Davenport replied.

Stone opened a file she had brought and pulled out the photograph of Dominick Winters. Holding it up, she said, "You remember this fella, don't you?"

"Yeah, that's the guy that owns the investment firm in Florida,"

"Correct," Stone said, "and guess what."

"What?" Davenport asked.

Stone replied, "It would appear that Mr. Winters' business opened shop about thirty years ago."

Stone then pulled out a picture of the now deceased Reginald Harrington from his obituary in the paper and said, "Now look at him."

Davenport put the photos side by side, let out a long whistle, and said, "They do look alike, that's for sure."

Smiling from ear to ear, Stone said, "Now, what if I told you that Reginald's oldest son Theodore disappeared in a supposed plane crash not long after Jonathon Blackwood was murdered."

Davenport's eyes widened as the thought struck him, "Are you saying that you believe Dominick Winters and Theodore Harrington are the same person?"

"We believe so, and if we're correct, that means that Beatrice Harrington either is now or helped in the past to harbor a fugitive, and we can go in there and get him because there's no statute of limitations on murder."

"And in doing so, gives us access to the property and everything else we may discover in the process," Davenport replied with a smile.

"Exactly!"

"What do you need from me?" Davenport asked.

"We need to know everything you can find out about the plane Theodore Harrington was on when it supposedly disappeared."

Davenport replied, "I can make that happen. It may take some time, but I can do it. As he got up from the conference room table, Davenport looked at Stone and said, "Let me get to it, and I will call you as soon as I know something."

Without another word, Davenport left the conference room, and as soon as he walked out, Stone looked at Clayton, knowing full and well what he was thinking, "Don't even say it!"

Clayton smiled, put his hands up in an innocent gesture, and replied, "Say what?"

Boone giggled at the two, then asked, "Ok, what's your next move?"

Clayton thought momentarily and replied, "I think we need to go back and talk to the coroner."

As soon as Stone heard what Clayton wanted to do, she looked at him with a slight grin and said, "Oh, really now. Do tell."

Ignoring Stone, Clayton said, "Hopefully, she can give us some insight into Peter Harrington's death."

Stone watched Clayton pull out his phone and dial, taking his phone off speaker.

After hearing King answer her phone, Clayton said, "Hello, this is Detective Clayton. I was wondering if Detective Stone and I could come over and talk to you about another death that could be connected." After a moment's pause, Clayton continued, "His name is Peter Harrington, and he died sometime before Jonathon did ... yes, I'll wait."

While Clayton was apparently waiting for the coroner to pull up the case, Stone smiled and whispered, "And just how is it that you happened to have her number in your phone?"

At that time, King must have returned on the line because Clayton replied, "That's fantastic. My partner and I will be right over. Thank you."

As Clayton hung up the phone, he looked at Stone and said, "Let's go."

Boone chuckled and said, "You're not going to answer her?"

"Nope," Clayton replied with a slight grin.

IT TOOK MORE than twenty-five minutes due to traffic, but Clayton and Stone finally arrived at the coroner's office and walked in. The secretary smiled when she saw them walk in and said, "Miss King has been expecting you. Go on back."

Clayton pushed the door open when it buzzed, and they walked back to King's office. "Hey, you two. It's nice to see you again," King said warmly as she looked at Clayton.

"You too," Clayton replied with a smile, "were you able to find the file on Peter Harrington?"

"Actually, I was and immediately noticed something very peculiar."

"What was that?" Clayton asked.

King asked, "Remember when I told you the last time you were here that my mentor was a man named John McMillian?"

"Yes, we remember," Stone replied.

"I am certain that this report was not done by him. It's very sloppy, and some of the injuries are inconsistent with the typed notes. Not to mention, look at the signature. It's signed John McMillian, but it's not his signature. I'm one hundred percent certain this coroner's report was forged."

"That's just great," Stone said, shocked. "Now what? Can we talk to McMillian and see who may have forged it?"

"No, I'm afraid he died several years ago," King said, "as far as who did it, it could have been any number of people at the time, and they simply put McMillian's name on it, knowing it would never be questioned."

"So, somebody was paid off," Clayton muttered.

"Looks like it," King said, "and considering it happened thirty years ago and we're just now finding it out ... I doubt that we'll ever know who exactly it was that was paid off."

Stone asked, "Could we exhume the body and do another autopsy?"

"Sorry, no, the remains were cremated afterward," King replied sadly.

"Great," Clayton muttered, "we have no way to know what happened to Peter Harrington."

"Damn," Stone said. Just then, her phone rang, and as she saw who it was, an ever-so-small smile crept across her face.

"Special Agent Davenport, I presume," Clayton said.

Ignoring Clayton, Stone picked up the phone and said, "This is Detective Stone ... not a problem, we'll be right there."

"That was quick," Clayton replied.

"Yep, that was Davenport, and he has something for us. He wants us to meet him back at the office."

"This sounds interesting," Clayton said.

"Not sure, he wouldn't say on the phone. I guess we'll find out," Stone replied.

## 13

Later that afternoon, Special Agent Davenport met with Clayton and Stone at their office. As soon as they saw him, both detectives knew he had found something good for them. "I take it you found something," Stone said as she smiled at Davenport.

"It took some digging, but I sure did," Davenport replied with a devious smile, "As it turns out, the Harrington family was more connected than we first thought."

"And how's that?" Clayton asked.

"As it turns out, Theodore Harrington may not have been aboard the plane that went missing off the coast of Florida."

Stone asked, "How did you find this out?"

Davenport replied, "Turns out, the aircraft that Theodore Harrington was supposed to take to Miami didn't have the range to get there, so it had to make a refueling stop along the way. It stopped in Melbourne on the coast and took off again, skirting the coast on the way down to Miami."

Clayton shrugged and said, "So, it made a pit stop. What does that prove?"

"Nothing by itself, but after taking off again and skirting the coast for a while, it heads out to sea, where it issues a mayday and disappears somewhere between Freeport in the Bahamas and West Palm Beach."

"Again, we know that much," Clayton said, "tell us something we don't know."

Davenport smiled devilishly and said, "Ah, but you don't know this interesting tidbit. I did some digging, and it would seem that the pilot was able to retire shortly after that, where he lived on Freeport and passed away fifteen years ago."

Stone sat there for a moment and said, "So, you're thinking he was paid to crash his plane? That seems a little outlandish. Don't you think?"

"Not if the money was good enough for him to retire," Davenport replied.

Clayton said, "So, the theory is that Theodore Harrington got out at the refueling stop and never got back on."

Stone picked up on what Clayton was saying and added, "And if that's true, I-95 runs straight down the Florida coast to Miami. Getting there from Melbourne would not be hard, especially if nobody's looking for you. If you have a new identity at this point ... from then on, Theodore Harrington simply vanishes with the plane, and Dominick Winters shows up in Miami."

"A slight oversimplification but more or less accurate. And get this," Davenport said, "when he was rescued after the crash, the pilot was asked what happened to his passenger. The pilot stated his passenger made it out of the plane, but large swells soon separated them, and he never saw him again, which, all things considered, is not out of the realm of possibility."

Everyone was silent momentarily, and then Clayton said, "We need to look into the investment firm run by Mr. Winters."

"I already have," Davenport replied, "and you won't believe what I've found."

Stone replied, "Let me guess ... the Harrington family is their only client."

"Not really," Davenport countered.

"What do you mean?" Clayton asked.

Davenport said, "On a hunch, I had one of our forensic accountants take a look at the situation. He happens to be a genius, by the way. It didn't take him too long to figure out what was happening."

"Which is what?" Stone asked.

Davenport replied, "Mr. Winters has quite a few legitimate accounts, but several other accounts appear to be a string of shell corporations in the Cayman Islands and Switzerland, of all places. These shell corporations then buy real estate in the Caymans. After holding onto the real estate for a time, these fictitious shell corporations then sell the real estate to another shell corporation and deposit the money into a bank in the Cayman Islands, thereby making legitimate deposits, at least on paper."

"From there, what happens to it?" Clayton asked.

"There have been regular withdrawals from the Cayman account, all under the $10,000 limit, to a Swiss bank account that was set up nearly forty years ago."

"Can we find out who has access to the Swiss account or how much money we're talking about?" Stone asked.

"We're still working on it, but it could take some time. The Swiss have relaxed their privacy laws in recent years, but it still takes time to cut through the red tape," Davenport said.

"That means we're screwed then," Clayton groaned.

"Not necessarily," Stone said with a devious smile.

"What are you thinking?"

Stone smiled and said, "If we go after Dominick Winters, he'll lawyer up and simply say that he's not Theodore Harrington. I'm sure by now, he'll be able to prove he is who he says he is legally. And if that's true, we don't have enough to compel him to give us a DNA sample, BUT what if we could identify him as being Theodore Harrington? The courts would have to compel him to give us a DNA sample."

Davenport caught on and said, "And that will get us in the door of the Harrington estate. Everything out in the open from then on is fair game!"

"Exactly," Stone replied enthusiastically.

Catching on to what Stone was saying, Clayton shot back, "We show William Harrington the picture and see if he can identify his supposedly long-dead brother."

"We're forgetting one thing, though," Stone replied.

"And what's that?" Clayton asked.

"We don't know where Winters' location is at the moment. He could be on the estate, or he could be back in Florida, the Caymans, or anywhere for that matter."

Clayton thought for a moment and asked, "Do we have a phone number for Winters Investments?"

"Yes, we have the number. Why?" Stone asked as she searched through some papers for the number and handed it to Clayton.

Instead of answering Stone, Clayton picked up the phone and dialed the number to Winters Investments. Stone listened while Clayton asked in a business-like manner, "Is Dominick Winters available?" After a brief pause, Stone heard, "Oh, he's vacationing in North Carolina? When do you expect him back? Next week ... perfect. Thank you."

After Clayton hung up the phone smiling, "Stone said, "It still doesn't prove that Winters, aka William Harrington, is on the estate."

Clayton replied, "For all we know, he is still there. We can execute a search warrant based on that fact and search every room on the property."

Davenport said, "You know you will only get one shot at this. If for some reason William can't or won't identify Theodore ... we're screwed."

Clayton replied, "Yeah, but it can't be helped. I say we put it all out there for William and show him. He moved all the way to California to get away from them for a reason. That means he's a good man and didn't want to be a part of what was happening. That's gotta count for something."

∾

TWENTY-FIVE HUNDRED MILES AWAY, William Harrington was just sitting at the table for a bite to eat when he heard a knock at the door. Setting his sandwich on the plate, Harrington got up and walked to the door. When he opened the heavy wooden door, he saw the same Crescent City police officer standing there, "Officer Hernandez, I can't say I'm surprised to see you again."

Hernandez smiled and replied, "I'm afraid someone needs to talk with you again."

"Very well," Harrington said. "Give me a moment to put my sandwich in the refrigerator."

"Sure thing," Hernandez replied as he stood on the front porch.

A few moments later, Harrington walked out onto the porch and closed his front door, ensuring it was locked before they left. "Ok, let's get this over with," he said.

After the short ride to the Crescent City police station, Harrington was again greeted by Detective Grant and escorted into the same conference room they were previously in. "All right, what do they need now?" Harrington asked as he shook hands with Grant.

"We will find out together," Grant replied as he dialed into the video call.

Once everyone was connected, Grant and Harrington saw the screen at the end of the table change to once again see the South Carolina detectives sitting there. Harrington saw Stone and Clayton wave at him, and then Clayton said, "I'm sorry to have interrupted your day again, but we have one other thing we would like to ask you."

Harrington smiled and said, "That's no trouble. What would you like to know?"

Clayton replied, "I am going to show you a photograph, and I want you to tell me if you recognize the person in the photo."

Harrington chuckled and said, "I'll try, but, as I've said, I haven't been back to South Carolina in years."

Harrington watched carefully as Stone opened a manila file folder sitting in front of her on the table, pulled out a photograph, and held it up to the camera, saying, "Do you know this person?"

Harrington leaned in closer to the screen and after staring at the screen for a moment, asked, "Where did you get this picture?"

Clayton replied, "We don't want to say because we don't want to lead you. Just please answer the question. Do you recognize the person in the photo?"

Harrington muttered, "It can't be ... it just can't be possible."

"What can't be possible?" Clayton pressed.

"It ... it looks like my brother Theodore, but it can't be. He's dead," Harrington said, staring at the screen as if he'd seen a ghost. "He died in a plane crash years ago. I was told his body was never found."

Clayton replied, "There could very well be a reason for that. This picture is of a man named Dominick Winters. He owns and operates an investment firm in Miami, Florida. Have you ever heard of him or Winters Investments before?"

Still staring at the picture on the screen of Dominick Winters, Harrington stuttered, "No ... no, I have never heard of either one before, but I'm telling you, the person in that photograph is a dead ringer for my long-lost brother Theodore."

Clayton said, "Tell me this, then Mr. Harrington—Do you ever remember hearing about a Swiss bank account?"

Harrington sat there for a moment, rubbing his chin, and said, "I remember father saying he had one for international travel, but I couldn't tell you anything else about it. I can't imagine it's still active. Why are you asking about an old account in Switzerland?"

"No reason. Let's get back to the photograph. How can you be sure that this person in the photograph is your brother Theodore?"

Harrington took a deep breath and said, "Detective Clayton, a man knows his own brother when he sees him. I can't offer you verifiable proof, but I am as certain as the nose on my face that my brother is in that photograph."

"That is what we were hoping you would say. Thank you, Mr. Harrington."

Before anyone could say anything, Stone, who had been listening to the conversation, said, "You don't seem to be terribly surprised that your brother is alive."

Harrington took a moment to choose his words and responded, "Detective, nothing about that family surprises me anymore. That is why I moved out here earlier in life. I wanted to stay as far away from that mess as possible."

"Well, it would seem you made the right decision," Stone replied, "thank you for talking with us again. Your insight has been invaluable."

"You are quite welcome, detective, and so you know, I will be heading out of town later in the day on a much-anticipated trip, so if you require anything else, you will have to reach me on my cell phone."

"Sounds nice. Taking a vacation?"

"Yes, actually. I am leaving in the morning to go to Wyoming for a week to see the Yellowstone National Park and the Grand Tetons." William replied with excitement in his voice.

"Well, have fun, and we'll try not to disturb you while you're on vacation."

William replied, "That would be most appreciative. Now I must be off. I have to finish packing."

Stone and Clayton looked on as William Harrington waved goodbye at them, stood up, and moved out of frame. After that, the screen went black as the call ended.

# 14

After ending the conference call with William Harrington, Davenport, standing out of frame listening to the interview, said, "Now it's time to get a warrant."

Clayton glanced at Stone and said, "Let's get started."

As they left the conference room, Davenport followed Clayton to his desk, and as they walked, Davenport said, "Just so we're clear, the murders are yours. Once we get in the door, my main concern is the artwork and seeing if I can put this whole Erebus debacle to bed once and for all."

"I understand completely," Clayton replied. As they walked up to Clayton's desk, he saw a list of names on a printout, "hello. What's this?"

An office worker walking around passing out various papers heard Clayton and replied, "That just came for you by courier from the Harrington Estate."

Clayton looked at the list of twelve names and said to Davenport, "This is the list of people that work on the Harrington Estate."

Davenport looked the names over and said, "Half of the names are of Spanish origin. What do you want to bet they are illegal or only have a work visa?"

"No bet," Clayton replied with a smile. He pointed to the first name on the list and said, "I want to start with that guy."

Davenport looked at the name and read, "Samuel Webb. Why him?"

"He was there the other day when Stone and I paid a visit to the estate. After Mrs. Harrington decided she didn't want to talk to us anymore, she had a man named Sam show us to the door. Not to mention, he was packing heat. If I had to guess, he is the family's muscle, and if Anna was killed because of something she saw or found out on the property ... he's at the top of my list."

Davenport said, "Let's divide and conquer. I'll take this list of names and run them while you and Stone get the paperwork for your warrant ready."

"Sounds like a plan," Clayton replied, "but before I get started, we need to talk to Chief Boone and see if we can make this happen first thing in the morning. If so, hopefully, he can get us a few extra bodies. I have a feeling we're going to need them."

Clayton and Davenport walked to Boone's office and stood in the open doorway until he finished with the phone call he was on. When he hung the phone up, Boone said, "What do you two need?"

"We have enough to move on the Harrington Estate, and I want to see if you can get us a couple of extra people, considering the estate is so large."

"Boone thought for a moment, and before he could say anything, Davenport replied, "I can always get some of my guys to come to lend a hand."

"That won't be necessary," Boone replied, "I have the manpower. I just want to be certain all of our ducks are in a row because I'm sure the Harrington family has some pretty expensive lawyers on retainer."

"We will make sure everything is correct, and I will be there as backup if something doesn't go as planned," Davenport replied.

"When do you want to go?" Boone asked.

"First thing in the morning. Bright and early," Clayton said with a devious smile.

"Okay, I'll set it up. Let's get everyone together here in the conference room at five o'clock in the morning. Take as much time as you need between now and then, making sure every T is crossed and I is dotted on the paperwork."

"Will do," Clayton and Davenport replied before leaving Boone's office.

As the two walked back to Clayton's desk, Davenport said, "You know this whole case hinges on the identification of one man who is over two thousand miles away. Don't you?"

"Yep, I know," Clayton replied.

"Do you also know if William Harrington is wrong, and we execute a search warrant on the Harrington Estate and Dominick Winters turns out not to be Theodore Harrington ... we're all going to be out of a job?"

"I know that too," Clayton replied.

"Sooo what are you going to do if you're wrong?"

Clayton gave Davenport a sideways grin and simply replied, "Retire."

BEFORE THE SUN came up the following morning, Clayton, Stone, Agent Davenport, Chief Boone, and six other officers piled into the conference room, where the strong smell of coffee waffled through the room.

Once everyone was seated, Boone stood up and said, "Good morning, gentlemen."

Stone barked a loud coughing noise, "Ah, Hem!" to the giggles of the men in the room.

"My apologies ... lady and gentlemen, I stand corrected," Boone said with a sideways smile. "This morning, our target is a singular person on the Harrington estate." Boone put the picture on the projector from Anna Blackwood's phone and said, "This is Dominick Winters. We believe he is also Theodore Harrington, who was supposed to have died in a plane crash off the coast of Florida thirty years ago."

After letting that sink in for a moment, Boone said, "Clayton, would you care to explain it from here on out?"

Clayton stood and said, "Certainly. Thirty years ago, we believe Theodore Harrington killed Jonathon Blackwood over a land deal that went south. Just a few short months before Jonathon Blackwood was found murdered, Theodore's youngest brother Peter was found dead under mysterious circumstances. We now believe that Theodore killed both Peter and Jonathon, and the family came up with the ruse of Theodore's plane crash to help him escape. We have a court order to get DNA from Mr. Winters. Suppose it turns out that Winters is, indeed, Harrington. In that case, we will return for Beatrice at a later date for harboring a fugitive at the very least. Now, I'm going to turn the briefing over to Special Agent Peter Davenport of the FBI."

Davenport stood up, introduced himself, and said, "To piggyback on what has already been said, the FBI also believes that the Harrington money comes from a criminal enterprise, namely multiple art thefts from the late fifties and early sixties, and that is where the family's money originates. We also believe the now-deceased patriarch of the family, Reginald Harrington, was the art thief who went by the name Erebus. With that being said, we are especially interested in artwork and, in particular, an 8mm handgun that was rumored to be on the property and was the murder weapon for Jonathon Blackwood thirty years ago, as well as Anna Blackwood just a few days ago. Are there any questions?"

One of the extra officers Boone procured for the raid asked, "What kind of a handgun is an 8mm?"

"Good question, and the short answer is we're not entirely sure. Our best guess is a World War II Japanese Nambu Officer's pistol. In short, if you see any handgun of any kind, secure it. Are there any other questions?"

Another officer asked, "Is anyone on the property armed, such as security we'll have to deal with?"

Clayton replied, "One man named Samuel Webb appears to be the family's security person or bodyguard. He is known to have a Colt .45 auto. He is an Army veteran, and get this, he did a stint in a rehab unit in California after his time in the Army. He will likely stick near Beatrice, the family's matriarch, since she writes the checks."

Boone said, "If there aren't any other questions, let's mount up and move out. I want to rendezvous about a mile down the road from the Harrington estate, where we will be met by two technicians who will get us through the electric gate at the end of the driveway. We will hit the lights and enter the property when that gate opens. Let's roll out."

Forty-five minutes later, the caravan of four vehicles stopped roughly one mile down the road from the entrance of the Harrington estate, where they waited for the technicians to override the electric gate.

Within moments of pulling to a halt on the side of the road, a work truck with two men in coveralls pulled up. After conferring with Clayton for a minute or two, all of the vehicles rolled silently down to the entrance of the estate and the electric gate spanning the massive driveway.

Within five minutes of stopping at the gate, Clayton, Stone, and Davenport smiled as they watched the metal gate silently open and swing out of the way.

As soon as the gate opened far enough for them to get through, Clayton and the other vehicles in the caravan activated their lights and sped onto the estate. Soon enough, the red and blue lights of multiple police cars danced off every surface near the driveway as they slid to a stop and quickly spread out, surrounding the main house to prevent any chance someone would escape.

Within minutes of getting onto the property, the main house was surrounded, and Clayton and Stone were banging away on the front door.

It took several minutes, but finally, one of the house staff personnel opened the door and said, "I must insist that you stop all that racket at once! Mrs. Beatrice is still asleep."

Stone snapped back, "That is not an option; now step aside or go to jail! Your choice!"

As the person who opened the door stepped aside to let Stone and Clayton enter, Stone said, "This is a warrant that allows us to search the property and collect a DNA swab from Mr. Dominick Winters. Where is he?"

The house staff stuttered and said, "He's ... uh,"

"Where!" Clayton shouted.

About that time, none other than Sam Webb came stomping around a corner and shouted, "What in the hell is going on here?"

"We're executing a search warrant; now stay out of the way or go in cuffs. Your choice," Clayton snapped.

"It's not even six o'clock in the morning yet!" Webb shouted.

"Surprise!" Clayton replied.

About that time, from the top of the stairs, everyone heard, "What is the meaning of this?"

Everyone stopped what they were doing in the entranceway of the main house and looked up at the top of the stairs to see Beatrice Harrington standing there with a full-length satin robe on.

"I'm sorry, ma'am," Sam said, "I tried to stop them, but they have a warrant to search the property."

"This is preposterous! I'm calling my lawyer right now!" Beatrice snapped.

"You might want to because I have a feeling you're going to need him," Clayton replied.

"What are you babbling about?" Beatrice snapped.

"You're at the very least harboring a criminal!" Clayton snapped back at her.

"What are you talking about?" Beatrice yelled as she slowly came down the stairs.

"Dominick Winters! Where is he?" Stone snapped.

Beatrice blurted out, "He's not here!"

About that time, Boone walked in and said, "I want this entire place searched! Round up every person in this house and put them in the living room."

Before they started, one of the officers came in with an older man and said, "This person was in the guest house out back. He was scrambling to load his car when I came across him."

Clayton approached the man and said, "Well, well, well, if it isn't Mr. Winters, or should I say Theodore Harrington. Where were you going in such a hurry?"

The man scoffed and said, "My name is Dominick Winters, and I am a friend of the family and here on business. I overslept and was due to catch a flight from the Columbia Metropolitan Airport this morning. I have to get back to my business in Florida."

"Well, you're not going anywhere for a while," Clayton replied, "considering you are one of the main targets of my search warrant."

"What in the hell are you talking about?" Winters replied.

Clayton reached into a jacket pocket, produced a DNA sample kit, and said, "Dominick Winters, I have a warrant to collect a DNA sample from you."

"And if I refuse?" Winters asked.

"It's court-ordered. You can't refuse. I mean, you could try, but we'll just take you into custody and have a nurse come to the station and forcibly draw blood from your arm. Either way is fine with me, but you are going to comply, one way or another," Clayton said with a devious smile.

Winters glanced around the room, then momentarily made eye contact with Beatrice and said, "Well, that's what you're going to have to do because I do NOT consent to any DNA swab."

Clayton smiled and said, "Very well, as you wish. Turn around. You're under arrest."

After placing handcuffs on Winters, Clayton sat him down in a chair and watched as Boone, Stone, and the others, including Davenport, searched the house from top to bottom.

"Really, I don't know what you think you're going to find," Beatrice sneered as she sat on the couch.

"I think you know exactly what we're looking for," Clayton said as he glared back at her. Where are the paintings?"

"What paintings? Beatrice shot back.

"You know exactly which ones I'm talking about. Look around. Your husband made a huge amount of money stealing precious works of art and selling them on the black market.

Beatrice snarled, "My late husband—"

"Was a crook and a thief," Davenport shot back, interrupting her.

"HOW DARE YOU! Besmirch the name of my husband like that!" Beatrice shouted.

"Pretty easily, actually," Davenport shot back with a sly smile.

"All right, everybody calm down," Boone told Davenport and Beatrice Harrington as things started to get heated between the two.

While two other officers kept a close eye on the people in the living room, everyone else searched the entire main house from top to bottom. After several hours, everyone met at the main house's front door, where Boone quietly asked, "Did anyone find anything referring to a gun or stolen paintings?"

Everyone in the search party shook their head, indicating that nothing was found other than Winters himself. Davenport whispered to Clayton and Boone, "You mean to tell me we have nothing except for Winters."

Frustrated, Boone looked from Davenport to Clayton and Stone and replied, "It appears that way."

Reading their body language, Beatrice smiled devilishly and said, "I told you there were no paintings."

Thinking momentarily, Boone pointed at Winters and said, "Put him in a car, and let's take him back to the station."

As Winters was pulled off the chair where he was sitting and led out the front door, Beatrice shouted, "Don't worry about anything! I'll have my lawyers meet you there."

Stone escorted Winters to the second car, ensured he was secure, and returned to the car she came to the estate in. As all the vehicles pulled out, Stone asked, "How could we have gotten it so wrong?"

"I don't know," Clayton said, "but we need to find out."

## 15

After getting him out of the vehicle and as they walked Winters to an interrogation room, Winters said, "I invoke my right to counsel. I want a lawyer."

"Don't worry, Mr. Winters. I'm sure your lawyer is already on the way," Clayton said as he rolled his eyes at Stone.

"And so is a nurse to draw your blood since you don't want to give us a cheek swab. Or have you changed your mind?" Stone asked.

"I will never consent ... lawyer!" Winters snapped.

"Very well then," Clayton said as he uncuffed Winters from behind his back, sat him down, re-cuffed him to a bar on the desk, and walked out, leaving Winters alone in the room.

Now standing outside in the hallway, Boone and Davenport walked up. Davenport spread his arms wide and asked, "What in the hell was that? Where were the paintings or the gun?"

"I'm not sure. All the evidence tells us that the paintings are there. We must have missed a room or something."

"Well, you need to figure out what it was because right now, we don't have squat," Davenport snapped before turning and angrily stomping off, saying, "I gotta go let my boss know what's going on."

"He's not wrong," Boone said.

"I know, but the photos of the artwork from Anna Blackwood's phone were geotagged from inside the estate. They have to be there."

"So, now, what are we going to do?" Stone asked.

Clayton thought momentarily and said, "We must have missed a room or something."

"We checked every room," Boone shot back.

"Did we?" Clayton asked, "Maybe there was a room we didn't see. Let's look at those photos again before Harrington's lawyer or the nurse shows up."

Clayton returned to the interrogation room and transferred Winters to a holding cell while Stone and Boone went to her computer to pull up the photos again.

As soon as Clayton met with Stone and Boone, Stone looked at him, smiled deviously, and said, "Look at this."

"What am I looking for?" Clayton asked.

Boone replied, "Look at the background, not the paintings. The paintings are on very light cream or white walls, with normal height ceilings and no windows. I never saw a room like that."

"Son of a bitch!" Clayton snapped, "We missed a room somewhere!"

"But where?" Stone asked. We searched every room."

"Or so we thought," Clayton replied as he rubbed his chin, "I have an idea."

"Which is what?" Boone asked.

"I hate to do it, but we need to talk to William Harrington again."

"Wasn't he going on vacation, though?" Stone asked.

"Yeah, but it can't be helped. Unless you want to try and explain it to Davenport when he gets back that we missed an entire room somewhere."

"Pass," Stone smirked, "make the call."

Clayton walked over to his desk, where he had the phone number for William Harrington's home and cell phone. First, he tried calling his home phone directly, and when he didn't pick up, he tried his cell phone, making sure to put the call on speaker so Stone and Boone could also hear the conversation.

On the third ring, Clayton heard William Harrington's voice say, "Hello."

Clayton said, "Good morning, Mr. Harrington. I'm sorry to call so early, but I have news and am desperate for more help. I hope I haven't caught you at a bad time."

"It's a little early, but because of my trip, I was already up. What kind of help do you require?"

"Mr. Harrington, at first light this morning, we executed a search warrant on your family's estate. We took Mr. Winters into custody for the time being until we could get a DNA sample from him so we could either identify or rule him out once and for all as being Theodore Harrington."

"And if it turns out that Winters is my brother, what then?" Harrington asked.

"Well, in that case, he will have quite a bit of explaining to do, but there is another reason why I've called so early. As part of the search warrant, we were looking for any artwork that could be there and a specific weapon we didn't find. Is there any place on the estate where there may be a room with no windows and a normal-height ceiling?"

"Actually, there is. Did you happen to find my father's old office?"

"We never saw an office," Clayton replied.

Harrington chuckled and said, "It's no wonder, you see, my father's office was hidden. It was made to look like a bookcase. A person could walk right by it and never know it was there."

Stone and Boone's eyes widened on hearing this, and before either one of them could say anything, Clayton asked, "How do we get in?"

Harrington said, "It's simple. If you're standing in front of the bookcase, on the right side of one shelf is a black book with silver lettering that says EREBUS on the spine. Tilt it back as if you were pulling it off the shelf, and it will open right up."

Clayton was unable to contain himself and said, "Thank you so much! You've been a huge help. I will let you know how it all turns out."

"Please do," Harrington said, "Now, if you will excuse me, I am going through security at the airport now. Have a good day."

"Of course, and have a good trip!" Clayton said as he hung up the phone.

"Holy shit! Did you hear that!" Stone said wild-eyed, "We missed an entire room!"

"Yeah, not to mention the name on the book!" Clayton said excitedly. He looked at Boone and said, "Boss, we gotta go back out there! Those paintings are there! I know it! If we can get back out there, we can put this whole thing to bed before lunch!"

"Agreed!" Boone replied, "Call Davenport and get him back here. He's going to want to be in on this!"

"Will we need another warrant?" Stone asked.

Boone thought momentarily and said, "Yes, I'll get to work on the warrant and run it out to you, lights and sirens if needed. Just get out there before something disappears."

"Done!" Stone said as she and Clayton headed for the door, "Stone looked at Clayton and said, "I'll call Davenport on the way and have him meet us out there. It will be faster."

Clayton shot back, "Agreed. We gotta get back out there in case the family gets nervous and decides to move the paintings. Right now, the paintings and the supposed murder weapon are the only things we have as leverage, considering we don't know yet that Winters is Harrington."

As Stone and Clayton walked quickly to their car, Stone asked, "Suppose we go back out there, and the paintings and weapon are not there. And what about Winters? What if he is who he says he is?"

Clayton replied, "I don't even want to think about it."

THIRTY MINUTES LATER, detectives Stone and Clayton met Special Agent Davenport at the front gate of the Harrington estate and were surprised to find that the gate was still open.

"Just us three this time?" Davenport asked.

"That's it. Boone wanted us to get back out here in a hurry in case the Harringtons tried to move the paintings." Clayton said.

"Ok, well, what are we waiting for? Let's go." Davenport replied.

Davenport and Clayton hit their lights and tore off down the long driveway, stopping as close to the main house as they could. All three instantly jumped out of their cars and bolted for the front door.

Davenport reached the door first and pounded the solid door with his fist. In a moment, one of the house staff opened the door and, without acknowledging them, simply turned and yelled that the police were back.

Shortly afterward, the three were met by Sam Webb and Beatrice Harrington, who bellowed, "What is the meaning of this? First, you come before the sun comes up, waking everyone up, and now you come back again before ten o'clock! What's going on with Dominick Winters? Where did you take him?"

Davenport replied, "Ma'am, Mr. Winters is in a holding cell at the Lexington County Sheriff's Department, awaiting someone to draw his blood. In the meantime, we realized we missed a room, and now we're back. Step aside."

Sam stepped forward and said, "Not so fast. Where's your warrant?"

Clayton stepped closer to Sam to the point where their noses almost touched and said, "Right now, we have probable cause. Now step aside or go in cuffs. Choose the second option ... please."

Sam grinned and slowly stepped aside, letting Clayton, Stone, and Davenport pass. "I'm calling my lawyer again! This is nothing more than harassment!" Beatrice snapped.

Ignoring Beatrice, in the meantime, Clayton, Stone, and Davenport walked over to a bookcase they had walked directly passed several times earlier that morning and never noticed.

As the three stood before the bookcase, Clayton pointed at a book and said, "There it is."

Seeing what they were looking at, Beatrice roared, "YOU CANNOT DO THIS!"

Not wanting to give away the fact that they had talked to William

Harrington, Clayton said, "Oh, yes, I can. You see, I didn't realize it at the time, but it's all making sense to me now." Clayton pointed to the black book on the shelf with EREBUS on the spine and said, "This book is the key. Isn't it?"

"This is preposterous! Beatrice snapped as she glared at Clayton, "Do not touch that book! It was my husband's!"

Clayton looked at Beatrice, smiled deviously and reached up and pulled the book back just as William Harrington said. While they watched, the bookcase swung inward, revealing a whole entire room.

While everyone was focused on the bookcase swinging open, Sam Webb bolted for the front door and started bounding down the steps. Momentarily caught off guard, Davenport and Clayton gave chase while yelling for Stone to stay there with the room.

By the time Clayton and Davenport had made it outside, Webb was down the steps and running around the front of the house toward the back of the main house where the cars were kept.

"He's making a break for it!" Davenport shouted to the trailing Clayton.

"Did you learn that at Quantico?" Clayton yelled back in between, taking huge gulps of air, trying to keep up with the younger Davenport.

As Davenport got to the front corner of the main house, he slowed and drew his weapon before turning the corner out of sight of the trailing Clayton.

With Webb and Davenport out of sight of Clayton, who had yet to get to the front corner of the house, a series of shots rang out. Clayton paused at the corner of the house, pulled his service pistol, and yelled, "Davenport! Are you ok? Davenport!" After not getting a response from the FBI agent, Clayton took a deep breath and charged around the blind corner.

As Clayton rounded the corner, he saw the prone figure of Davenport on the ground. Writhing in pain but could not see Webb anywhere in sight. Clayton ran to the stricken Davenport to check his condition.

Kneeling beside Davenport, out of breath, Clayton huffed, "Where are you hit?"

Through gritted teeth and struggling to catch his breath, Davenport replied, "Took a round ... in the vest ... can't breathe."

Before Clayton could check to see if the round penetrated Davenport's vest, Clayton heard a car crank up in the nearby three-car garage. Momentarily turning his attention from the wounded Davenport, Clayton saw one of the estate cars accelerating out of the garage with Webb behind the wheel, speeding toward them and the estate entrance.

Clayton quickly stood, aimed, and fired several rounds at the vehicle as it sped out of the garage. Clayton fired several shots through the front windshield. One of his well-aimed shots had the desired effect as Clayton saw Webb's body jerk and slowly fall forward onto the steering wheel. Clayton watched as the car slowed, veered off course, and coasted until it came to a halt against a centuries-old oak tree.

Turning his attention back to Davenport, Clayton released the Velcro on either side of Davenport's vest and cautiously lifted the body armor away from his chest and was relieved to find not a drop of blood. The round fired by Webb did not penetrate Davenport's chest plate.

Clayton sighed in relief and said, "It didn't penetrate." Clayton lifted Davenport's shirt, saw a huge purplish-blue color on the right side of his chest, and said, "You probably have a broken rib or two, though."

Again, through gritted teeth, Davenport replied, "Gee! Ya think?"

Clayton said, "You're lucky. You just took a .45 round to the chest plate. Don't try to talk. You could still have internal bleeding." Clayton took the radio off his hip and put the officer down call, over the radio.

Immediately, Stone came bolting around the corner with her weapon drawn and advanced on the car now stopped against the tree. Stone reached in and felt Webb's neck for a pulse. Not finding one, she ran to check on Davenport, who was still down on the ground.

As she knelt down beside Davenport, Stone was somewhat relieved to see that Davenport was at least conscious. By this time, several house staff personnel came running around the corner with pillows and blankets to help the stricken FBI agent. Knowing that Davenport's injury was not critical, Stone and Clayton left him in the care of the house staff while they raced back into the house to take Beatrice into custody and search the room they had previously missed.

By the time Stone and Clayton started retracing their steps back inside the main house, they heard multiple sirens headed in their direction. Clayton then put it over the airways to slow the responding officers down because the situation had been brought under control.

## 16

When Clayton and Stone walked back into the main house, they found Beatrice sitting on the couch right where she had been left, seemingly indifferent to the exchange of gunfire outside. When the detectives returned to the house, Beatrice scowled at them and said, "My lawyer is on his way."

Clayton smiled deviously and replied, "Good, because if I find what I think I'm going to find in that room ... you'll need him."

Clayton and Stone stepped into the darkened room, and after feeling around, Stone managed to find a light switch just inside the door and turn it on.

Stone gasped at the sight before her as soon as the light came on. Clayton and Stone were standing in the doorway of a room that was the size of a typical master bedroom except for one significant distinction.

At eye level, at one-foot intervals, all the way around the room, were priceless works of art by various master painters. Stone's eyes widened as she said, "Holy shit! Look at this room!"

"I can't believe what I'm seeing," Clayton said in amazement.

"No shit!" Stone replied excitedly as she walked around the room, looking at several pieces, reading off some of the painters' names,

"Monet, Degas, Renoir, and a few others that I can't pronounce and haven't heard of before. Some of these paintings have to be worth millions."

"Tens of millions, probably," Clayton said, shocked as he walked toward the only piece of furniture in the room, an elaborate desk and an equally elaborate plush chair.

"These paintings should be in museums for everyone to see, not locked up here. Where did they all come from?" Stone asked.

"I'm not sure, but maybe we can find some information in the desk," Clayton said as he sat behind the desk.

Before Clayton could pull open a drawer and look around, they heard Beatrice's sneering voice coming from the doorway, "Where's your warrant? You can't open that without a warrant!" She roared with a tinge of panic in her voice.

"As I told you when we got here, probable cause says that I can," Clayton snapped.

"I'll keep an eye on her," Stone replied as they heard sirens blaring as cars barrelled onto the estate.

After resigning herself to the fact that she couldn't stop the detectives from looking inside the desk, Beatrice glared at Clayton and said, "Go ahead if you must. It won't do you any good anyway. Everything is written in my husband's shorthand. He taught it to me years ago in the event something happened to him, but I'm not telling you how to read it."

Stone smiled and said, "Sounds like you just made yourself an accomplice," as she spun Beatrice around and put her in cuffs.

"I did no such thing!" Beatrice snapped as Boone and several other officers came bounding up the steps and into the house.

Clayton looked up at Boone and said, "We found it, but Davenport took a bullet to his chest plate from Webb, Beatrice's head of security, when he went to make a break for it."

"Yeah, I checked on him on the way in. He's up and in the ambulance already. He's good," Boone replied," I also have a new warrant, so we're good. I added a tidbit about getting DNA from Beatrice, also."

"Beautiful," Clayton said with a smile.

Stone had an officer escort the now handcuffed Beatrice back into the living room and onto the couch while Clayton put on a set of nitrile gloves and cautiously opened the drawers on the desk one by one.

When he opened the desk, Clayton found several files and notebooks, all of which were written in a type of coded shorthand. "It all looks like gibberish," Clayton said to Boone as he walked over to join Clayton at the desk. As he shuffled some notebooks around, he also came across several business cards with one word printed on them ... Erebus. "BINGO!" Clayton said with a smile.

"What do you want to bet that those business cards are exactly like the ones Erebus left at his robberies? Maybe Davenport's people can help with it," Boone said.

Before Clayton could answer, they heard, "Did ... I hear my name?"

Boone, Clayton, and Stone looked up to see Davenport leaning against the doorway. "You should be in the ambulance headed to the hospital!" Clayton snapped.

"Yeah ... but I had to see ... the room first," Davenport slowly said as he held his ribs and tried to take short breaths.

Stone walked over, slowly put her arm around Davenport for support, and said, "Back to the ambulance you go, mister."

As Stone slowly guided Davenport back out of the room, Clayton and Boone heard Davenport tell Stone, "Ya know, if it weren't for the whole gunshot and broken ribs thing ... I'd be in heaven right about now."

As they stepped outside the hidden office, Boone and Clayton giggled as Stone replied, "Shut up and focus on your breathing. I'm making sure you get in the ambulance this time. Boss, I'm going to ride with Davenport to the hospital and make sure he's okay."

"Not a problem," Boone said as he and Clayton chuckled at Stone. As Clayton pulled open the bottom drawer, he said, "Hello, there!"

"What is it? Boone asked.

Clayton carefully reached into the drawer with a pen and slowly produced a very old and unknown type of handgun that resembled a World War II German Luger but was obviously different.

Examining the gun closely, Clayton saw a serial number stamped on one side, and upon carefully turning the weapon around, he saw several small, stamped characters that appeared to be Japanese writing.

As soon as he saw the characters, Clayton smiled and said, "Whatcha want to bet that this is an 8mm Japanese Nambu?"

"No bet," Boone replied, letting out a long whistle."

"This has got to be the murder weapon, and I'll bet that when it goes to the lab, we're going to find Webb's fingerprints on it." Clayton surmised.

"That's a fair guess, but wouldn't he have worn gloves or at least wiped it down after killing Anna Blackwood?" Boone asked.

"He should have, but you know just as well as I do that criminals always miss something."

Boone replied, "Yep, well, I gotta get everybody in here, crime scene, SLED for the shooting, and FBI's probably going to show up sometime because one of their agents got shot, not to mention, we're probably going to need their help on the shorthand."

About that time, both men could hear Beatrice yelling from the other room, "Wait until my lawyer gets here! You're not taking anything until he sees the paperwork! I want everything inventoried!"

"And somebody get her out of here!" Boone snapped.

Moments later, Boone got a phone call and left the room. He returned moments later and said, "Nurse just took Winters' blood. I put a rush on it, so we should know the truth soon as if we don't already know."

"Yep, and I'll be willing to wager a week's salary that I know whose fingerprints will be on the gun also," Clayton said.

"No bet there," Boone replied, "but speaking about guns, you need to meet with the SLED shooting team and hand over your weapon to them for the investigation. I know it was a good shoot, but according to policy, you'll be on desk duty until the investigation ends."

"I know. It's not my first shooting," Clayton said.

"Go ahead, the shooting team is waiting to talk to you," Boone said.

∽

IT TOOK the rest of the day and into the night to make sure the house staff was interviewed, and everything in the hidden office was cataloged and entered into evidence.

By the time Clayton talked to the SLED shooting team and returned to the station, there was a proverbial army of lawyers already there arranging for Beatrice's and Winters' release.

When Clayton finally reached his desk, he found Stone sitting there, going through a mound of papers found on the estate. "How's Davenport?" Clayton asked.

Stone sat back and rubbed her eyes for a moment, and said, "It's pretty much what we thought. He has one broken rib and one cracked rib. He will be hurting and riding a desk for a while, but otherwise, he'll be okay. How did things go at SLED with the shooting team?"

"That's good, and the interview with the shooting team went fine. Of course, I'm riding a desk until the investigation is over, but I was quietly told that it's a formality at this point. What's going on?"

"Well, several lawyers showed up and immediately started the paperwork for Beatrice's release. They also tried to spring Winters, but after Boone talked to a judge, he managed to get Winters held until the bloodwork comes back at least."

"That's good. We don't need him going anywhere just yet because I have a feeling that as soon as that bloodwork comes back, he will have some explaining to do."

"We don't have anything to match Winters DNA to, though. Do we?" Stone asked.

Clayton thought for a moment, smiled, and said, "Technically speaking, no, but he doesn't know that. Let's see if we can use that to our advantage. Have someone put Mr. Winters in one of the interview rooms. I want to talk to him."

Stone replied, "Will do, but first, I want to show you what I've found. Look at this paperwork. This is a bank statement from a company called Aether LLC in Wyoming to Webb in the amount of fifty-thousand dollars. I also found emails on Webb's phone through an anonymous emailing service stating that once confirmation the job was complete, the rest will be sent."

"Well, I'll be damned!" Clayton replied, shocked, "No wonder Webb tried to take off. Someone paid him to kill Anna Blackwood."

"But who and, more importantly, why?" Stone asked, "This whole case is so confusing."

"It is, but we're almost to the end. I just need to have a conversation with Mr. Winters."

"I'll call down and have someone put him in an interview room," Stone said.

Detective Clayton made sure the video and audio recordings were working, walked into an interview room ten minutes later, and sat at a table across from Dominick Winters.

"What is going on? When can I leave?" Winters asked.

Clayton replied, "You're not going anywhere for a while, I'm afraid, Mr. Winters. Or should I say ... Theodore Harrington? Your blood test results have come back, and imagine our surprise when it came back that you are indeed Beatrice Harrington's son."

In that moment, Winters' entire demeanor changed. He dropped his head and stared at the table, then looked into Clayton's eyes and said sadly, "I can't do it anymore."

"Do what?" Clayton pleaded.

"Live a lie," Winters muttered as he buried his face in his hands.

Smelling blood in the water, Clayton seized the opportunity and said, "What lie? Talk to me. You know you will feel better if you let it all out. Did you kill Jonathon Blackwood? Is that what all this is about?"

Upon hearing this, Winters looked up at Clayton with pain in his eyes and said, "You really have no idea. Do you?"

Clayton said, "We're still putting the puzzle together, but we don't have all the pieces yet. Talk to me so we can figure this out."

"I never hurt anybody. I could never do anything like that. Being the oldest, I was raised to protect the family name and protect my siblings at all costs. That sort of thing. Also, as the oldest, I was privy to certain details about the family that the others didn't know about."

"What sort of things?" Clayton asked.

Winters took a deep breath, exhaled slowly, and said, "My father was ... well, he was basically a fence for stolen artwork."

Clayton interjected, saying, "He was more than a fence for stolen artwork. He was the one doing the stealing. Have you ever heard the name Erebus?"

"Yes, as I'm told, that was the name my father went by in the art world."

"That's partially correct," Clayton replied, "you see, in the late 50s and early 60s, there was an exceptionally good art thief responsible for dozens of art thefts. This thief always left a calling card with one word on it ... Erebus."

"Is that where my family's wealth came from?"

"As far as we can tell, yes," Clayton replied as he saw the wheels spinning in Winters' head. "But what I want to really know is this. How did we get here? More importantly, how did *you* get here as Winters?"

Clayton watched as Winters deflated before his eyes from a strong-willed man to a mere shell of the person he was when he came into the room. Taking a deep breath, Winters said ... it's true. I'm Theodore Harrington, or rather I was. That person is all but gone now. I'm about to tell you something no other living soul knows."

"Go ahead, I'm listening," Clayton replied softly.

"Earlier in life, my brother had an issue for a time with ... drinking, and we all knew it. It became the dirty little secret of the family. There was a lot of sibling rivalry between Peter and William. When Peter and Jonathon Blackwood came up with this plan for the land deal ... William became extremely upset because he wanted to be a part of the deal. Still, because of his drinking, he was erratic, to say the least."

"Are you saying what I think you're saying?" Clayton asked.

"That William killed Peter ... yes. That's exactly what I'm saying. The night Peter died, all three of us, myself, Peter, and Jonathon, met up on the dirt road to watch the sunset over the plot of land we were planning to buy. William knew where the plot of land was and knew we were going to meet up there."

Clayton said, "Go on, you're doing great."

Winters took a deep breath and kept going, "William showed up drunk, as was the norm back then, and he and Peter got into an argument about the money and not allowing William into the deal. Peter tried to do the right thing and take William's keys, but they fought, and William got back in the car and tried to take off. At the last second, Peter jumped in front of the car in an attempt to stop William from leaving, but instead of that happening ..."

"William hit Peter," Clayton said, finishing Winters' sentence.

With tears running down his face, Winters could only nod his head up and down. At about that time, the interview room door opened, and someone produced a bottle of water for Clayton to give Winters, which he gladly accepted.

After Winters thanked Clayton for the water, Clayton said, "Okay, so how does that get you here where you are with me?"

Winters said, "After we checked on Peter, it became obvious that he was dead. I told Jonathon to leave and never speak about what he saw, and I would take care of everything. I called Father, who rushed out to where we were. Being the influential person my father was at the time, he knew the right people to make it go away quietly."

"Ok, I get that part, but I don't understand how that led to everything else happening," Clayton prodded.

"After the funeral, my father said the best thing to do would be to keep appearances going, and that meant continuing with the land deal even though Mother disapproved, so that's what we did. Not long after that, Father went on one of his business trips to Atlanta, I think, to acquire an art collection, as I remember. Anyway, while he was away, William took the gun Father brought back from the war and killed Jonathon to keep the secret from getting out."

"How do you know this, exactly?" Clayton asked.

"I know this because my father told me that to protect the family name, he and mother had come up with this scheme to have me disappear. Nobody outside the family except Jonathon knew of William wanting to be in on the deal." Winters said. "When my father got back from his trip to Atlanta and found out what happened to Jonathon, he knew William was behind it, but to outsiders, I was the only one of the three out of the deal that was alive."

"So, you became the fall guy for your brother, but you got a new name, identity, and business out of the deal," Clayton said in shock.

"Correct, and in return for doing this, I get the financial backing of the family's apparently ill-begotten wealth, and my brother William, who caused all this in the first place, was essentially removed from the family. On top of that, when both mother and father passed, the majority of the family's wealth was to be donated to my business ... namely me."

Now, in total shock at how far the family was willing to go to protect the family name, Clayton asked, "And when you say William was essentially removed from the family, you mean what exactly?"

"Father had him sent to a rehab facility in California where it was discovered that he had sociopathic tendencies, and that's why he drank so much. Once he cleaned up his act and started getting help for his sociopathy, father set him up with a generous ... allowance, if you will, as long as he stayed in California."

Clayton said, "Tell me about Webb then. What did he have to do with everything?"

"I'm not sure. He was a recent addition to the estate. Why?"

"Because, after checking into Webb's background, looking at his phone, we discovered a payout in the amount of fifty-thousand dollars from an obscure LLC in Wyoming, and with Wyoming laws being what they are, the LLC is completely anonymous. We also discovered an anonymous email with a promise to pay the remaining amount when the job was done."

Winters asked, "Was the company in Wyoming called Aether LLC?"

Clayton's eyes widened with surprise as he replied, "How did you know that?"

Winters replied, "Because, in Greek mythology, Aether was the son of Erebus."

"So, if you now live and have a business in Florida, how is it that you were on the estate before Anna was killed?"

"Mother reached out under the guise of needing to do business with me in person. When I arrived, she told me confidentially that there was a rat on the estate and wanted my help to find out who it was. Before I could start poking around ... Anna was murdered."

Clayton asked, "How did she know there was a rat?"

"Because she told me that one of the paintings in my father's old office was slightly askew as if someone had bumped it, and she was the only person at the time who knew of the room, which meant that someone other than her had been in there. She wanted me to find out who knew about the room and what they knew."

Clayton sat for a moment writing notes, then asked, "Do you have any proof of what you're telling me?"

Winters smiled devilishly and said, "Of course."

"What kind of evidence do you have?" Clayton asked.

"The night Peter died, I had the idea of bringing a camera to take a photograph of the sunset over the land we were going to get. There are several photographs taken at the scene just before and just after Peter died. William was so wasted I don't know how much he remembers that night. I wouldn't be surprised if he didn't even remember the camera. The film is in a safe in my office in Florida."

Clayton said, "Ok, let me talk it over with my boss and coworker, and we'll go from there."

Clayton stepped out into the hallway, and Stone stepped out from the observation room next door wild-eyed and said, "I can't believe what I just heard. If what Winters says is true, Webb was working for William Harrington, and William had Webb kill Anna to keep from discovering the truth."

"But if that's true and William has been in California this entire time, how did William even know about Anna?" Clayton asked.

"She must have tracked him down and reached out to him," Stone said.

"And the minute she did ... her fate was sealed," Clayton replied sadly.

"You know what this means now?" Stone asked.

"Yep, we gotta find William Harrington," Clayton said, "and we need to pressure Davenport to find out about that Swiss bank account also."

"We have his number. Let's give him a call," Stone said.

"Who? Davenport or William Harrington?" Clayton asked.

"Both, actually," Stone said, smiling.

# 17

Across town, FBI Agent Davenport was sitting up in a private hospital room after being treated for blunt force trauma inflicted by Webb's gunshot to his bulletproof vest. His phone started to ring, and ever so slowly, he reached for his phone and, after seeing the name on his caller ID, answered saying, "Aw, did you call to check on me?"

Stone giggled and said, "Yes ... and no. First off, how are you doing?"

"Docs say I'll be okay soon enough. There was no internal damage to organs, just my ribs," Davenport replied.

"That's good news," Stone said, "now, on to the real reason I called."

"Man, talking about no sympathy and cutting someone to the bone," Davenport smirked.

"Yeah, well, some of us are working and not lying in bed all day," Stone replied.

"It's not like I got shot or anything," Davenport said with a pained chuckle, "Oh, don't make me laugh. It hurts."

"Anyway, back to the real reason I called. Were you or someone at the FBI able to help us with the Swiss bank account?"

"Yes and no," Davenport said, "the particular bank that this account was in has very strict privacy requirements, and all they would tell us was it was connected somehow to an Aether LLC in Wyoming—"

Stone's eyes widened, and before Davenport could even finish his sentence, Stone said excitedly, "Son of a bitch! I gotta tell Clayton!"

"I take it you've heard of Aether LLC before?" Davenport asked.

"Sure have, and it's not good!" Stone said.

Stone hung up the phone and raced down the hallway to tell Clayton what Davenport had said on the phone about the Swiss account now being linked to Aether LLC.

As soon as Clayton found out what Davenport told Stone about the accounts being connected, Clayton snapped, "Harrington's running! He's not going to Yellowstone. He's going to clean out and shut down that Aether LLC!"

"Can't he do that online?" Stone asked.

"He can, but there has to be a reason he's going there. There must be a safety deposit box there with something he needs. We gotta move on this and move now."

As Clayton started walking quickly toward Boone's office, he heard Stone ask, "What do you want me to do about Winters?"

Clayton stopped, thought briefly, and said, "Cut him loose. Send him home to Florida with the knowledge that if he turns over the evidence he's holding ... we'll work out a deal and tell him the Miami police will be there to check and make sure he's doing what he's supposed to be."

"How will we find the bank where Aether LLC's accounts are?" Stone asked.

"We can't, but I'll bet the FBI can," Clayton said.

"I'll call Davenport again," Stone said.

"Wait, before you do, what happened with Beatrice? Is she still here?"

"No, she's gone; she's probably back on her estate by now; however, as a term of her release, she had to relinquish her passport."

"Good move," Clayton said, "now call Davenport back and tell him we need his help again ... bribe him with a date or something," Clayton said with a sideways grin.

As Stone pulled her phone out to call Davenport again, she said, "I'm going to pretend like I didn't hear that."

Clayton barrelled into Boone's office without stopping and said, "Boss, we need to talk."

"This can't be good," Boone replied.

After Clayton told Boone what was happening, he remarked, "When the FBI finds the bank, I want the local police to pick him up. That means I may need to make a little trip to take him into custody."

"Let's get him in cuffs first, then we'll work out the details," Boone said.

"Sounds good," Clayton said as he turned and walked back out of Boone's office to find Stone.

Clayton found Stone sitting at her desk holding the phone up to her ear when Clayton walked up, "What's going on?" he asked.

"I'm on hold. Davenport actually has one of his friends in blue-collar crime on the other line now, doing what they can. Stone glared at Clayton, saying, "You owe me big time, mister."

"Why's that?" Clayton asked innocently.

"I had to agree to go on a date with him if he could help us," Stone said.

"You know what that means?"

"No, what?" Stone asked.

"He already knows somebody who can find out for us. He conned you," Clayton smirked.

Davenport apparently came back on the line, and Stone said, "Let me know as soon as you know something ... yes I remember our deal."

On hearing this, Clayton grinned and let out a little chuckle. For this little slip, he was on the receiving end of a single-finger salute from Stone.

Moments later, she hung up and said, "It's going to take an hour, and he's going to call me back. So, what do we do in the meantime?"

Clayton couldn't resist taking another shot at Stone, chuckled, and said, "I happen to know that Davenport's favorite color is green."

Stone threw a stack of Post-it notes at Clayton, bringing him an even bigger laugh.

～

AN HOUR AND A HALF LATER, Stone's phone rang. She listened for a moment, then started writing something furiously on a piece of scratch paper. "Yeah, yeah, it took ya long enough," she said before hanging up.

"So, when's the date?" Clayton smirked.

Ignoring Clayton, Stone said, "Aether LLC's account is in a bank in Jackson Hole, Wyoming."

"We gotta get a move on because he already had a head start on us," Clayton said as he jogged off toward Boone's office.

Clayton bolted into Boone's office again and slapped a piece of paper in front of him, saying, "That's the target bank."

"I'll give Jackson Hole police a call right now and get them to send someone to check on it for us. You and Stone go home and pack a go bag. If Jackson Hole police can pick up William Harrington, I want you two on the next flight out to bring his ass back here in cuffs."

"Yes, boss," Clayton said with a smile.

Clayton went back to tell Stone the news, and they immediately went home to pack a bag in the hopes they would be flying out to Wyoming to pick up Harrington soon.

Thirty minutes later, while Clayton was packing a bag at his apartment, he received a phone call that stopped him in his tracks. It was Boone calling to say Jackson Hole police were too late, and Harrington had managed to close the bank account associated with the LLC and remove something from a safety deposit box.

Clayton plopped down on the bed, deflated, and said angrily, "Damn it! I knew it!"

After calming down, Clayton called Stone, who asked, "Now what?"

"I'm going to give Harrington a call. I will see if I can get him to make a mistake." Clayton said before hanging up with Stone.

Clayton dialed the number for William Harrington, and on the third ring, he answered, "Hello?"

Putting on the show of his life, Clayton said, "Mr. Harrington, I'm sorry to disturb you on your trip, but I was wondering if you could help me with something."

"It's quite all right," Harrington said, "what would you like to know?"

Clayton asked, "Is there a safe or anything like that on the estate you can recall?" Clayton was simply trying to get Harrington to talk, hoping he would either make a mistake or Clayton would hear something in the background of the phone call that would give away his location, and that's exactly what he heard.

As Harrington replied, "No, I don't recall there being a safe anywhere, but I haven't been to the estate in years," Clayton heard what he hoped to hear.

"Well, ok, thank you anyway. Hope you're having fun on your trip," Clayton said, seemingly going along with Harrington's ruse.

"Oh, I am!" Harrington replied. "Well, I must be off. There's much left to see. My next stop is Old Faithful!"

"Well, have fun," Clayton said as he hung up the phone. As soon as Clayton heard the click of the phone call ending, he snapped, "Bullshit!" Clayton immediately dialed Boone's number and excitedly said, "He's leaving Jackson Hole right now!"

"How do you know?" Boone asked.

"I just called him. He said he was heading out to the Old Faithful Geyser in Yellowstone, but I am positive I heard a boarding call for a flight in the background. He's at the airport right now!"

"I'll make the call to Jackson Hole police right now!" Boone snapped before hanging up.

As soon as the call ended Clayton called Stone to update her on the situation and that there was still a chance to catch Harrington.

Twenty minutes later, Clayton received a call from Boone saying

Jackson Hole police missed Harrington, but he held tickets on two different manifests, leaving within minutes apart.

"Where are they going?" Clayton asked.

"One flight is going to San Francisco, and the other is headed to Las Angeles. Boone replied, "I'll give both police departments a call now, but I don't know if we'll make it."

"Well, stop talking to me and start calling them!" Clayton snapped.

After hanging up with Boone, Clayton called Stone again and said, "Meet me at the station. I want to look over the evidence again."

"Why?" Stone asked.

"I think we missed something," Clayton replied.

∼

CLAYTON AND STONE met back at the station, and Stone asked, "So, what's this all about? Don't we know who's behind everything?"

"Most likely, but I just want to look at something again. For some reason ... something does not add up to me," Clayton replied, "besides, I need to keep busy until we hear if Harrington's in custody or not."

"What part isn't adding up?" Stone asked.

Clayton shook his head and said, "I don't know, but I have a hard time believing Harrington pulled all this off while living in California. He had to have help."

While they were pouring over all the evidence they had amassed from day one, Boone came to find them. They knew it was not good as soon as they saw his face. "What is it?" Clayton asked.

With a huff, Boone replied, "San Fran police missed him by thirty minutes. He already boarded another flight."

"Where to? Stone asked.

"Montenegro," Boone said with disgust.

"Clayton threw his pen on the desk and said, "That's it!"

Stone looked confused and said, "What's it? I don't get it."

Boone replied, "Montenegro does not have an extradition treaty with the United States. Harrington is as good as gone."

"There's got to be something we can do," Stone replied.

"I'm afraid not," Boone replied.

"Well, what about the money in the account? Can we seize it?" Stone asked.

"Seize the money in a Swiss bank. I highly doubt it," Boone replied.

At that moment, Clayton sat up and said, "Wait a minute!"

"Tell me you have something," Boone asked.

"Stone may be on to something," Clayton replied as he furiously began looking through papers on his desk.

"What are you looking for?" Stone asked.

"Transcript of Winter's interview," Clayton said as he shuffled papers.

Finally finding what he was looking for, Clayton quickly began scanning the transcript until he found what he was looking for, "BINGO!" he nearly shouted with excitement.

"What is it?" Stone asked.

"I didn't realize it at the time, but when Winters was in the interview room, *he* was the one who brought up the Aether LLC account."

"Ok ... so what?"

"Clayton smiled deviously and said, "How did he know about the account? That was a private account his father set up to send Harrington money. The only way Winters could have known about that was if Harrington told him! Winters had to be in on it the whole time!"

"We gotta find him and get him back here now!" Stone replied excitedly, "he's got some explaining to do."

Boone initiated a BOLO and started an immediate search for Winters, but he already had a huge head start. Boone immediately sent cars back to the Harrington estate and was surprised to find that he was not there. None of the staff had seen him, and all his belongings were still on the estate. Boone had a car stationed there in the event he should return, but it wasn't likely.

Soon enough, word returned from the Columbia Metropolitan Airport that, earlier in the day, Winters had boarded a flight to New York instead of returning to Miami.

"Damn! He's running, too!" Clayton said with disgust.

"I'm gonna check in with New York police and see if they can determine where he went at least, but I have a sneaky suspicion that I already know," Boone replied.

"Where?" Stone asked.

"Montenegro," Clayton said sadly, "they're both gone."

# EPILOGUE

Less than twenty-four hours after leaving the United States, the man known as Dominick Winters checked into an extravagant hotel in Podgorica, the county's capital of Montenegro. After being shown to his room, he paid the young man who helped him with his bags. The young man thanked Winters and promptly left.

Winters waited ten minutes before leaving his room, walking two doors down and knocking. It only took a moment for the door to open, but when it did, he was greeted by none other than William Harrington saying, "Welcome brother, it is so good to see you again."

After sharing a hug, Winters asked, "Did you send the package?"

Harrington smiled devilishly and said, "Yes, it's on its way. Before long, the police detectives working on the case will have everything they need."

THREE DAYS LATER, Stone kept her word and went on a date with FBI Special Agent Davenport, but only if Clayton would accompany the coroner Courtney King. Clayton fought it at first, but finally, he went along with the idea.

While they were all sitting around a corner table at the restaurant, King asked, "Okay, so fill me in on everything. How did all this take place?"

"That's going to take a while," Clayton said.

"Try me," King replied with a smile, "just the cliff notes version."

"Okay," Clayton said, "Several things are going on, but here goes. William Harrington did, in fact, have a problem with drinking. As far as we can tell, he did accidentally kill his younger brother thirty years ago."

"Ok, I'm up with ya so far," King replied.

"Beatrice was more concerned with the family name. It was all about the family name and status for her. Well, she couldn't have this getting out, so she made her husband pay some people off, and Peter's death quietly went away. The only outside person who knew the truth was Jonathon Blackwood."

Stone picked up from there and said, "After Peter's death, Jonathon was a liability and had to go. Beatrice made Theodore kill Jonathon to keep the family secret. Then Theodore had to go, so they invented the plane crash, making a new life for him while at the same time shipping William off to California. Problem solved … Until Anna Blackwood came nosing around with the idea to write her book."

"And from there, everything simply snowballed," Clayton replied.

"Exactly." Stone said, "Somehow, Beatrice found out about Anna's real name or about the book and decided she had to go. We may never know, but the assumption is Beatrice decided to silence Anna to keep the family's secret of Reginald being Erebus and the stolen art, not to mention where all the family's wealth came from. In reality, what got Anna killed had nothing to do with Jonathon Blackwood's murder."

"How did you figure all of this out if the two brothers got away?" King asked.

"Simple. After William Harrington started to run, he went to a bank in Wyoming, where he closed an account and emptied a safety deposit box. Yesterday, I received a package in the mail from Wyoming from William with all the evidence we need to put Beatrice away for the rest of her life. There was also a letter in the package addressed to me telling me that both brothers felt abandoned by the family for the sake of the family name and hatched a plan to get back at their mother."

"What about the brothers then?" King asked.

"There's nothing we can do about them, but at least we got Anna's killer in the name of Samuel Webb. When we explained it to Anna's family, they seemed to find some comfort in the fact that we would never have known about any of this if it hadn't been for her. As for the brothers, we've alerted INTERPOL, but all we can do is wait and see if they make a mistake like leaving the country.

"So, did you ever find out what was in the Swiss account?" King asked.

Clayton replied, "Oh, yes. Not long after both brothers arrived in Montenegro, the contents of the Swiss account were transferred into Bitcoin and poof; the money vanished into thin air."

"Dare I ask how much money we're talking about?" King asked.

Davenport piped in and said, "The Swiss finally got back to the FBI, and although they wouldn't say who transferred the money to Bitcoin, they did tell us it was roughly seventy-five million dollars."

"So, it's over then?" King asked.

"Yep," Davenport replied, "with that kind of bankroll, it's doubtful the brothers will ever leave Montenegro."

Clayton said, "It's over in more ways than one. The brothers are out of reach, Beatrice is behind bars, and I've worked on my last case. I put my papers in today."

After hearing that Clayton was officially retired, Davenport ordered a round of drinks and made a toast, "May you live in peace and quiet for the rest of your life! Cheers!"

Everyone at the table agreed, lifted a glass, and said, "Cheers!"

After the toast, Clayton leaned over, kissed King, and said, "Whadda ya say? You want to retire with me?"

Before Courtney could say anything, Clayton's phone rang. He glanced at the number and, recognizing the call originated outside of the United States, decided to answer, "Hello?"

After a slight delay, Clayton heard, "Greetings from Montenegro, Detective Clayton. I trust you got the package in the mail I sent you?"

Shocked, Clayton replied, "Yes, I got the package, and you will be glad to know that your mother will be spending the rest of her life behind bars."

By now, the table was dead silent as everyone listened to Clayton's side of the conversation. "I don't understand why you set your mother up like that," Clayton said.

William chuckled and said, "It's simple. That old hag took everything from my brother and I for the sake of the family. She ruined the first part of our lives, so it's only fitting we ruined the last part of hers. If you happen to see her at her trial, do tell mother we appreciate her keeping the Swiss bank account all these years and that Montenegro really is nice this time of year. If you're ever in this part of the world, detective ... please look my brother and me up. We'd love to have you over for dinner."

"Somehow, I don't think that's going to happen," Clayton said, "I'm retired," and with that, he hung up the phone.

Davenport asked, "Was that who I think it was?"

"It sure was," Clayton replied."

"What are you gonna do?" Stone asked.

Clayton held his hands and said, "Nothing ... I'm retired."

# ABOUT THE AUTHOR

Steven Jacobs was born in 1971 in Wilmington, North Carolina, and at an early age, he became interested in all aspects of history. He became a history buff by watching old movies with his father that contained great actors such as Cary Grant, John Wayne, Henry Fonda, Steve McQueen, and many others.

Later in high school, Steven excelled in United States history, especially in the turbulent years of the early to mid-1900s, and this is where his love for military history flourished. By the time Steven was thirty-five years old, he had read countless books on United States history with a focus on the era of World War II.

At the age of forty-five, he wrote his first book about the disappearance of a German U-boat in World War II called The Disappearance of U-491. Steven had such a wonderful time writing his first book that he continued writing and, to date, has just finished his fourteenth book.

Now, at the age of fifty-three, Steven lives in Columbia, South Carolina, and he has worked for the government for fifteen years.

Please 'like' and follow his Author's Facebook page for updates and sneak peeks at other books in the works. Amazon reviews and anywhere else that takes book reviews are always appreciated!

www.ingramcontent.com/pod-product-compliance
Lightning Source LLC
Chambersburg PA
CBHW050451110726
47899CB00003B/899